# MACAQUE ATTACK
## NATURE'S NIGHTMARES, BOOK 1
## STACI LAYNE WILSON

Excessive Nuance

# PROLOGUE

The macaques had not always called the twisted mangroves of Florida home. Their history began over four decades ago when Paramount Pictures transported thirty-seven crab-eating macaques from the Philippines to the swampy outskirts of the Everglades for the filming of *Jungle Fury*—a box office disappointment that the studio preferred to forget. When production wrapped, the decision was made: returning the animals was too costly, so the handlers simply released them into the unfamiliar wetlands, assuming that nature would take its course.

Nature did, but not as expected.

The creatures—resourceful, intelligent, and adaptable—did not perish; they thrived. Generation after generation learned to navigate the strange new ecosystem, developing behaviors their ancestors never needed on the shores of Southeast Asia. Where they had once stripped the sweet flesh from bananas and jackfruit, they learned to catch the slow-moving crabs that scuttled along the tepid shoreline and survive on birds' eggs, insects, and whatever they could find in garbage cans and dumpsters.

What began as a frightened, disoriented troop soon developed into a complex society. Hierarchies formed and reformed. Territories were established, defended, and occasionally abandoned for more promising grounds. Young males were exiled and formed satellite colonies, while matriarchal lines strengthened through successive births. The macaques developed their own culture, one neither fully wild nor domesticated, but uniquely adapted to their peculiar circumstances as ecological immigrants.

Alpha had not been born with his name or his rank. Both had been earned through decades of cunning, strength, and—most importantly—patience. At twenty-three years old, his silver-streaked fur and scarred face told the story of countless challenges overcome. Now, perched on a high branch of a cypress tree, he observed the strange, upright creatures whose ancestors had brought his ancestors to this land.

The two-legs never ventured too deep into the macaques' territory. They carried small rectangular objects that flashed light, pointed them at the troop, and made excited sounds. Sometimes they left behind colorful wrappers containing sweet things. Alpha had long ago taught the younger ones to wait until the humans departed before investigating these offerings.

Today, something was different. The two-legs had brought large, metal things that bit into the earth. They wore bright clothing and spoke with loud voices that scattered the birds. Alpha watched with unblinking eyes as they marked trees with bright orange ribbons—including the ancient banyan where three generations of his family had slept. He didn't understand their purpose, but instinctively, somewhere in his genetic memory, he recognized the pattern from many seasons ago, when the humans had last encroached this far.

Alpha bared his teeth silently as a breeze carried unfamiliar scents through the canopy. The colony had faced threats before—hurricanes, drought, pythons, and rival troops. But the approaching danger felt different. Alpha could not name it, yet he sensed it in his bones. Something was changing in their world, and he would need all his wisdom to lead his family through what was to come.

# CHAPTER 1

D r. McKenna Dubrow's hands were steady as she removed the final cactus thorn from the whimpering bulldog's muzzle. Basil—a barrel-chested male with a surprising capacity for both trouble and patience—belonged to Hank Webster, whose strawberry farm supplied half the county with berries and the other half with stories about his eccentric farming methods.

"There we go, buddy. All done." McKenna stroked Basil's broad head as his stump of a tail thumped against the examination table. "Forty-seven spines total. That's got to be some kind of Cypress Grove record."

Hank, a wiry man with sun-weathered skin and perpetually dirt-stained hands, shook his head. "Fool dog never learns. You'd think after the first time..."

"Maybe he thinks he's part porcupine and is just trying to grow his own quills," McKenna said, preparing a syringe of antibiotics. "Though I'm not sure the cactus appreciated being used as a donor."

She administered an injection with second-nature ease, Basil barely flinching under her gentle touch. The bulldog looked up at her with mournful eyes that seemed to communicate both regret and a strange pride in his misadventure.

"I'm sending you home with pain medication. Monitor the puncture sites for infection."

Hank nodded, absently scratching behind Basil's ears. "Appreciate it, Doc. What're the chances he'll do it again next week?"

McKenna capped the used needle and disposed of it in the sharps container. The familiar click of the lid closing punctuated her thoughts. She'd seen Basil through three such incidents in the past year alone. There was something almost comforting about these routine emergencies—predictable, solvable problems with clear solutions. Unlike her previous work.

"I'd say about as likely as the sun rising tomorrow," she replied with a chuckle, writing instructions on Basil's chart. "Some lessons just don't stick."

As Hank looked over the instructions, McKenna considered the dog's predicament. Animals operated on instinct, curiosity, and past experience—a combination that sometimes led to repeated mistakes. Humans weren't much different, she reflected, thinking of her own tendency to take on more responsibility than she could reasonably handle.

The clinic door chimed, and McKenna heard her receptionist Marjorie greeting someone, followed by her daughter's voice responding with the monosyllabic efficiency of a teenager acknowledging an adult's existence without inviting further conversation.

"Kira's here," she remarked, unable to keep a note of surprise from her voice. Her daughter rarely visited the clinic voluntarily.

"That little gal still designing dresses?" Hank asked, folding up the paperwork and putting it into his back pocket.

"Fashion is her passion," McKenna said with a bland smile. "She's applying to design programs in New York next year."

"Long way from Florida," Hank observed.

"That's part of the appeal," McKenna replied, helping Basil down from the examination table. The unspoken remainder of that thought—*getting away from me*—lingered in her mind as she led dog and owner into the reception area.

Kira sat in the corner chair, her short, bobbed hair catching the afternoon sunlight streaming through the window. Her slim fingers moved rapidly over her phone screen, a slight frown of concentration on her face. Today she wore a floral-patterned jumpsuit that McKenna vaguely recognized as something ordered online last month, paired with chunky platform sandals that added three inches to her height.

"Hey, Kira," McKenna called out. "Didn't expect to see you here."

Kira looked up, her expression flickering between annoyance and something more vulnerable before settling on neutral. Her large, wide-set eyes seemed to change color constantly, reflecting hazel or grey, and sometimes green, depending on the light. McKenna's own eyes were a pale blue, but mother and daughter shared the same fine, silky blonde hair. "Dad called. Video chat in twenty minutes. Wi-Fi at home is being weird again."

McKenna nodded, ignoring the familiar twist in her stomach at the mention of her ex-husband. Martin Dubrow was currently somewhere in Kenya, working with wildlife conservationists and living the unencumbered professional life he'd always wanted. The monthly video calls with Kira were his concession to parenting from afar.

"You can use my office," McKenna said. "Then we can head home for dinner."

Kira shrugged, neither accepting nor rejecting the offer of a shared meal, and disappeared down the hallway toward the office. McKenna watched her go, recognizing the graceful way she moved—so similar to her father's easy athleticism, so different from McKenna's own delicate efficiency.

Hank cleared his throat. "Teenagers, huh? My youngest just turned twenty-two, and I'm still recovering."

She smiled, turning her attention back to her client. "You're good to go. Call me if Basil develops any swelling or shows signs of infection."

After the pair departed, McKenna checked the appointment book over Marjorie's shoulder. "Am I done for the day?"

Marjorie, whose immaculate silver bob and reading glasses on a beaded chain belied her sharp memory and even sharper wit, tapped the screen. "Dr. Santos is handling the Cole's cat at four. You're clear until tomorrow's farm calls."

"Perfect. I can—"

The phone rang, and Marjorie answered with the clinic's standard greeting. Her friendly expression shifted to concern as she listened. "Yes... Uh-huh... Earl Simmons, yes... I understand... Dr. Dubrow is available now... Yes, we'll handle it."

McKenna raised an eyebrow as Marjorie hung up. "Earl Simmons?"

"Shot one of the macaques," Marjorie said grimly. "Sheriff's deputy is there now. They want you to come collect the body and determine cause of death, though it seems pretty obvious."

McKenna sighed. Earl had been a source of numerous animal-related complaints over the years, from shooting at neighborhood cats to allegedly poisoning raccoons. The macaques, however, were different—they weren't just wildlife but a tourist attraction and local mascots of sorts.

"I'll go now," she said, already calculating how this would affect her evening plans. "Let Dr. Santos know I might not be back before closing."

She walked down the hallway and paused at her office door, where she could see Kira setting up her laptop, adjusting the angle to capture the most flattering light.

"Kira? I have an emergency call. Will you be okay here until I get back?"

Her daughter barely glanced up. "Yeah, fine. Dad will probably talk for an hour about elephant migration patterns or whatever."

"Tell him I said hello," McKenna said automatically, though they both knew she didn't mean it.

"Sure," Kira replied, equally insincere.

McKenna grabbed her medical bag from the supply room and headed for her truck. The customized white Ford F-150 had been her biggest investment after the divorce—a mobile veterinary unit equipped with refrigerated storage, medical supplies, and specialized gear for field examinations. The truck represented both her independence and her commitment to serving Cypress Grove's animal population, regardless of where they were located.

As she drove through town toward Earl's property on the eastern outskirts, McKenna found herself watching the trees and rooftops more carefully than usual. The crab-eating macaques had been a fixture in Cypress Grove for as long as she could remember, their presence so normalized that tourists often expressed disappointment if they visited without spotting at least one. The monkeys generally kept to themselves, venturing into town primarily for easy eats in the dumpsters behind restaurants or to perform for tourists who would feed them despite the numerous signs advising against it. The residents had mixed feelings about their simian neighbors, but most understood that they were good for the local economy.

Earl's property came into view—a run-down ranch house surrounded by unmaintained land gradually being reclaimed by the encroaching forest. A sheriff's department vehicle was parked in the gravel driveway beside Earl's rusting pickup. As McKenna pulled in behind them, she spotted Deputy Collins standing on the back porch with Earl, both men looking at something on the ground.

"Afternoon," she called as she approached, medical bag in hand. "I understand we have a situation with one of the macaques?"

Earl Simmons—bony, perpetually scowling, and smelling faintly of cigarettes and beer even at three in the afternoon—crossed his arms defensively. "Damn right we do. Thing was breaking into my shed again. Third time this week."

Deputy Collins nodded in greeting. "Dr. Dubrow. Mr. Simmons called in reporting he shot a monkey that was damaging his property. Given the protected status of the macaque colony, we need to document the incident."

Her gaze lowered to the pitiful sight of the macaque's lifeless form sprawled across the yellowing grass that struggled to thrive in the stubborn patches of Earl's neglected lawn. The monkey was unmistakably a mature male, its robust physique and the well-defined musculature around its shoulders and arms speaking to a life of agility and strength. Its long, semi-prehensile tail, a hallmark of its species, lay limp and lifeless.

The macaque's fur, matted with the rusty stain of its own blood, covered in flies and gnats, bore the grim evidence of its untimely demise. From the congealing pool of crimson that seeped into the thirsty earth below, McKenna could see the devastating path of the shotgun pellets. The blast had torn through the animal's midsection with brutal efficiency, shredding vital organs and snuffing out its life in a single, painful instant. The sight was a graphic reminder of the fragility of existence, even for creatures as spirited and resilient as the macaques that roamed the outskirts of their small town.

McKenna felt a twinge of sorrow, mingled with frustration, at the senseless loss of life. As a veterinarian, she had dedicated her career to preserving it, and yet here she was, faced with the consequence of human impatience and a lack of understanding for the creatures that had long been part of their local landscape. The macaques, with their intelligence and complex social structures, had always held a special place in her heart, and the senseless violence inflicted upon this one stirred a sense of injustice within her.

She took a deep breath, steadying herself as she knelt beside the body, her professional facade sliding into place. She shooed the buzzing insects away with the sweep of one hand. "You couldn't have called animal control instead of shooting it?"

Earl spat to the side. "Called them twice before. By the time they show up, the little bastards are long gone. Then they tell me to secure my trash better, like it's my fault." He gestured toward six metal garbage cans lined against the house, now secured with bungee cords and concrete blocks. "I did what they said. Then they started breaking into my shed." He looked down at the corpse and shuddered in obvious revulsion. "Ugly fuckers, ain't they?"

McKenna took the question rhetorically, pulled on examination gloves, and gently turned the macaque's body. "What were they taking from your shed?"

"Tools, mostly," Earl said. "Wire cutters disappeared a few days ago. Hammer the week before. Thought it was kids messing with me until I caught this one red-handed, trying to get out with my good pruning shears."

Collins made a note in his report. "We've had similar complaints from three other residents in the past month. The macaques seem to be getting more... bold."

McKenna frowned, peering closely at the monkey's hands. The calluses didn't match the typical patterns she'd expect to see. These suggested repeated, precise manipulation of objects—more extensive than normal macaque activity would produce.

"I need to take the body back to the clinic for proper examination," she said, standing. "Where's the shed they've been breaking into?"

Earl pointed to a surprisingly solid structure standing apart from the house. "Over there. Put on new locks after the second break-in, but somehow they still got in."

McKenna walked toward the shed, noting the incongruity between its sturdy construction and the general disrepair of the rest of Earl's property. The door hung slightly ajar, and as she approached, she noticed something unusual about the wooden frame. "What are these marks?"

The deputy joined her, examining the series of parallel scratches on the door frame. They weren't random damage but appeared to form a pattern—three vertical lines crossed by two horizontal ones.

"Freaking apes did that," Earl boomed from behind them. "Noticed it after the first break-in. They're marking the places they hit, I figure."

"They're monkeys, not apes." McKenna studied the marks more closely.

Earl rolled his eyes. "Well, excuse me! They're a menace is what they are."

She pushed the door open wider and examined the interior of the shed. Tools hung on pegboard walls, each outline carefully labeled in fading marker. Several spaces were empty where tools should have been.

"How many tools would you say are missing in total?" she asked.

Earl shrugged. "Dozen, maybe? Mostly cutting tools, hammers. Had a coil of copper wire disappear, too."

The veterinarian stepped back outside, her unease growing. "I'll need to document all this."

As McKenna retrieved the office camera and a body bag from her truck, an unnatural stillness descended over Earl's property. The cicadas, previously humming in the afternoon heat, fell abruptly silent. Even the distant birdsong ceased, as though nature itself was holding its breath.

A prickling sensation at the back of her neck came on, then intensified—primal, instinctual—the feeling of being watched by something that understood watching. She turned slowly, scanning the tree line that bordered the property. The dense Florida foliage swayed in the afternoon breeze, but something was wrong about the movement—too deliberate, too coordinated, as though the forest itself had developed intention.

Then she spotted them—three macaques perched in the branches of an ancient oak tree, completely motionless except for their beady brown eyes. Unlike normal wildlife observation, their gaze wasn't merely curious—it seemed calculating, measuring, assessing. Their steady stare followed her every movement with an uncanny intelligence that seeped into her consciousness like frigid water.

The primates were positioned strategically among the gnarled branches, their tawny bodies almost camouflaged against the weathered bark. One smaller female crouched near the trunk, while two larger males had taken higher positions, creating what looked like a surveillance triangle. McKenna had observed countless wild animals during her veterinary career, but never had she felt so deliberately scrutinized. These weren't the random, scattered positions of normal troop behavior.

The macaques' tails hung loose and still, another deviation from their typical restless behavior. Even their breathing seemed synchronized, chests barely moving as they maintained their vigil. The largest one, perched on a thick branch directly above, tilted its head slightly when McKenna met its gaze—a subtle, almost human gesture of acknowledgment that sent a wave of goosebumps dashing down her arms. She recognized the patient vigilance in their posture, reminiscent of predators rather than the typically skittish, opportunistic foragers she knew them to be.

"Deputy," she called quietly. "Look at the large oak, about thirty yards to your right. Don't make any sudden movements."

Collins turned casually, then stiffened. A barely perceptible tremor ran through his hand as it moved instinctively toward his holster. "Well, we've got an audience."

"They're watching," McKenna said. "*Really* watching."

One of the macaques—larger than the others with a distinctive milky right eye and a long scar down its face—made direct eye contact with McKenna. The creature didn't simply look at her; it looked *into* her, as though cataloging her weaknesses. There was an unsettling wisdom in that gaze, an assessment that felt deliberately intimidating. The monkey's lips pulled back slowly, revealing yellowed canines in what could have been a threat display or, more disturbingly, something like a knowing smile.

Earl had noticed the observers, too. He took a step toward his house. "I'm getting my shotgun."

"No," McKenna hissed sharply. "That would be a mistake. Deputy Collins, please make sure Mr. Simmons understands that shooting another macaque would result in charges."

The officer nodded, moving to intercept Earl. "She's right, Mr. Simmons. One could be justified as protecting your property, but more would suggest intent."

"So what? They're animals. Vermin." But Earl's posture relaxed and he stayed where he was.

McKenna walked backwards, closer to the shed. Finally turning her back to the onlookers, she carefully placed the bloody, nearly bisected corpse in the body bag and sealed it. As she carried it to her truck, she could feel the eyes of the watching macaques following her. When she turned to look again, the one with the bad eye raised its hand in what looked like a deliberate gesture before melting back into the foliage with its companions.

"I'd recommend securing your house tonight, Mr. Simmons," McKenna called. "Windows, doors, everything. And maybe stay with a friend if you can."

Earl's face darkened, and he spat down into the bloodstain on his lawn. "You think I'm scared of some stupid-ass monkeys?"

* * *

The drive back to town took McKenna past the town square, where the weekend farmers' market was being set up. As vendors arranged their stalls and hung signs, McKenna noticed something un-usual—the square was completely free of macaques. Normally, market setup would attract at least a few opportunistic critters hoping for fallen produce or unattended snacks.

Instead, as she drove slowly past, McKenna spotted them on the rooftops surrounding the square—at least a dozen macaques posi-tioned on different buildings, watching the human activity below.

They weren't making noise or trying to steal food. They were simply... observing.

She took the long route back to the clinic, steering her truck down Cypress Avenue where bulldozers and construction equipment sat dormant in the late afternoon sun. The massive clearing, once a beautiful stretch of wetland pines, now resembled an open wound on the landscape—raw earth exposed where a shopping mall would soon stand.

COMING SOON: CYPRESS CREEK GALLERIA, the billboard proclaimed in garish orange letters. LUXURY SHOPPING, DINING, AND ENTERTAINMENT.

McKenna's grip tightened on the steering wheel. The mall represented everything that had drawn her to Cypress Grove in the first place—or rather, its opposite. After the divorce, she'd chosen this town specifically for its lack of chain stores, its locally-owned businesses, and the way nature infiltrated every corner. Cypress Grove had character; it had soul. Now, developers were carving it up piece by piece, paving paradise to put up a parking lot, just like the old song warned.

The construction site triggered memories of Miami—concrete sprawl, endless traffic, and the constant press of humanity. She'd spent six years at Zoo Miami with Martin, specializing in predator care. The work had been stimulating, even exhilarating at times, but the city itself had worn her down. The noise, the crowds, the artificial landscape—all of it had felt increasingly suffocating as the years passed.

She remembered the morning commutes through gridlocked traffic, the air conditioning battling against the humid heat, the constant vigilance required to navigate urban life. Her ex-husband had thrived on the energy, the chaos, the social connections that came with city living. She'd withered.

"And now it's following me here," she murmured, glancing again at the construction site.

The body bag containing the macaque shifted slightly in the refrigerated compartment behind her. Something about the incident with Earl nagged at her. The watching macaques, the tool theft, the markings—none of it fit with normal primate behavior. She'd need to perform a thorough examination and document everything properly.

As she turned onto Main Street, she caught sight of another crab-eating macaque perched atop the hardware store, watching the traffic below with unnerving focus. Unlike the playful creatures that had entertained tourists for years, this one sat with sniper-like stillness, only its eyes moving as it tracked her vehicle.

At the intersection near the high school, she spotted another small group in the parking lot. Three macaques appeared to be examining the underside of a parked car, one of them lying on its back and reaching up into the vehicle's mechanical components.

McKenna pulled over, watching with growing concern. After a moment, the macaque emerged from beneath the car holding something small and metallic. The three primates then moved with coordinated efficiency to another vehicle, where they repeated the process.

She reached for her phone to call the sheriff's Department when the macaque with the object—which McKenna now recognized as potentially a spark plug or similar part—suddenly turned and stared directly at her truck. It nudged its companions, and all three looked her way simultaneously. There was a moment of stillness before they scattered in different directions with startling speed.

McKenna's phone rang, making her jump. Vivian Santos' name flashed on the screen.

"Hey, Viv," she answered, still watching the now-empty parking lot.

"Where are you?" Vivian's normally calm voice held an edge of tension. "Marjorie said you went to deal with a shot macaque at Earl Simmons' place."

"I'm on my way back now," McKenna said. "I've got the body for examination. But Viv, I'm seeing some very unusual behavior from the rest of the colony."

"Like what?"

"Like coordinated observation. Tool use. Possibly tampering with vehicles?"

"What?" Vivian asked with a slight chuckle.

McKenna reached for her glove box and opened it. "Can I call you right back?"

Without waiting for a reply, she pressed the end-call button and, setting the phone down, she reached into the glove box and got out a small spiral-bound pad and pen. She wrote a note to the car's owner, explaining what she'd seen, and secured it under the windshield wiper.

She watched as a lone alligator ambled across the road, making it safely to the other side and disappearing into the switchgrass.

Deed done, she pulled back onto the road, accelerating toward the clinic. She hit redial and as soon as her colleague answered, she continued the conversation. "They're leaving symbols at every break-in," McKenna said. "It's a pattern."

There was a pause on the other end of the line. McKenna figured her partner was thinking she'd gone off the deep end.

Finally, Vivian said, "You should know that since you left, we've had three calls about macaque break-ins. The Hendersons, the Miller farm, and the hardware store."

McKenna felt a cold certainty settling in her stomach. "This isn't random. They're collecting specific things."

Viv laughed, but McKenna didn't. She wasn't kidding.

"Okay, but why?"

"I don't know," McKenna said, watching as another macaque darted across the road ahead of her. "But I think we're about to find out."

# Chapter 2

McKenna pulled into the clinic's rear parking area just as the sun was beginning to set, casting long shadows across the teal-trimmed building. She backed her truck close to the private entrance that led directly to the examination rooms, wanting to minimize any view of the macaque's body. Cypress Grove's relationship with its simian residents was complicated enough without adding a public spectacle.

She had just finished unloading the body bag when Vivian Santos emerged from the rear door. Vivian—thirty-four, with a practical bob of dark hair and round glasses that magnified her observant brown eyes—had joined the practice last year, bringing both specialized exotic animal experience and a no-nonsense pragmatism that complemented McKenna's more emotionally invested approach.

"Kira said you'd be back soon," Vivian said, holding the door open. "She left about twenty minutes ago. Said she was walking home to work on some design project."

McKenna nodded, hiding her disappointment. She'd hoped to catch the end of Kira's call with Martin, maybe even exchange a few civil words with her ex-husband. "How'd the Cole appointment go?"

"Urinary crystals, as expected. Got them started on the prescription diet and scheduled a follow-up." Vivian's attention shifted to the body bag. "So, this is our gunshot victim?"

"Adult male, shot by none other than our beloved Earl Simmons," McKenna confirmed, carrying the bag inside. "But there's more to this situation than a simple wildlife clash."

They walked through the back corridor to Examination Room 3, which was reserved for their more complex cases. Unlike the more cheerful rooms used for routine pet visits, this space was equipped with advanced diagnostic equipment, a larger stainless-steel examination table, and specialized lighting for surgical procedures.

"I asked Marjorie to call Sheriff Harding before she left," Vivian said, helping McKenna place the shattered body on the examination table.

McKenna unzipped the body bag to reveal the macaque's remains, the gunshot blast creating a stark contrast against the animal's gray-brown fur. Its wizened face was frozen in a death sneer, sharp fangs punctuating clenched teeth.

"I'll start the external examination while we wait for the sheriff," McKenna said, reaching for a pair of latex gloves. "Can you prepare the imaging equipment? I want full radiographs before we open him up."

"He's pretty much already opened up," Viv replied ruefully.

As Vivian set up the portable X-ray machine, McKenna began the methodical process of documenting the macaque's external condition. She photographed the body from multiple angles, paying particular attention to the entry wound and the animal's hands and feet. She measured and weighed the specimen, noting the results in her digital recorder.

"Male, approximately six years old based on dentition and development. Weight is 6.3 kilograms—notably heavier than typical for crab-eating macaques of comparable age and size. Muscle development is exceptional, particularly in the upper limbs."

McKenna gently extended one of the macaque's arms, examining the hand structure. "Significant callus development on both hands, inconsistent with standard foraging patterns. Calluses suggest repeated use of tools or mechanical manipulation."

She and Viv exchanged a puzzled glance, then she moved to the animal's head, carefully examining the facial structure and cranium. "Cranial capacity appears larger than standard for the species, though confirmation will require detailed measurement post-mortem."

The clinic door chimed, followed by heavy footsteps in the reception area. Moments later, Sheriff Lucas Harding's imposing frame filled the doorway. Even off-duty and out of uniform, Harding projected authority—six-foot-three with broad shoulders and a methodical manner that matched his no-nonsense law enforcement approach. Today, he wore faded jeans and—perhaps ironically, perhaps inadvertently—a vintage black concert t-shirt with Peter Gabriel's "Shock the Monkey" tour artwork faded across the chest. His cowboy boots added another inch to his already considerable height.

"Doc," he nodded at McKenna, then at Vivian. "Dr. Santos. Marjorie said we have a situation with the macaques?" His voice was deep, and his Panhandle drawl pronounced.

"Sheriff," McKenna acknowledged. "Thanks for coming. This goes beyond a simple shooting incident." She gestured to the examination table. "Earl Simmons shot this macaque breaking into his shed—the third break-in, according to him."

Harding approached, studying the body with professional detachment. "Deputy Collins filed his report. Said Earl claimed the monkeys were stealing tools?"

"Not just from Earl," Vivian interjected. "We've gotten reports of other break-ins across town. It's weird."

"We've documented some concerning anomalies," McKenna added, indicating the macaque's hands. "Look at these callus patterns. They're consistent with regular, purposeful tool manipulation. And the body weight is significantly higher than normal for this species. The muscle definition is more developed than I've ever seen in a feral macaque."

Harding frowned. "Could be they're just well-fed from tourist handouts, no? These monkeys have been living the good life in Cypress Grove for decades."

McKenna shook her head. "This isn't about diet, though that's unusual too. The physical development suggests coordinated activity. And there's something else." She recounted what she'd seen—the macaques observing from rooftops, tampering with vehicles, the uncanny marking system on Earl's shed.

"Sounds like they're getting bolder about scavenging," Harding said, though a flicker of concern crossed his face. "They've always been opportunistic little thieves."

Vivian had completed setting up the X-ray equipment. "We're ready for imaging if you want to step out, Sheriff."

"I'll wait in the hall," Harding said, moving to the doorway. "Wanna know what you find."

After capturing radiographic images from multiple angles, McKenna transferred them to the monitor while Vivian prepared instruments for the internal examination. They called Harding back in, and the three of them gathered around the screen as McKenna began analyzing the results.

"There's our entry wound," she indicated the shotgun damage. "Cause of death is obvious—massive trauma to the thoracic and abdominal cavities."

She moved to another image showing the cranium. "But look at this—the skull structure. The cranial capacity is approximately fifteen percent larger than documented standards for this species."

"What does that mean?" Harding asked.

"It means more room for brain development," McKenna said. "And look at the density patterns in the cerebral region. There's evidence of enhanced neural development, particularly in the frontal lobe—the area associated with planning, problem-solving, and complex behavior."

Vivian leaned closer to the screen. "That's not normal evolutionary development. Something accelerated this."

"Could it be natural adaptation?" Harding asked. "They've been isolated here for what, forty-five years?"

"That's a geological blink of an eye in evolutionary terms," McKenna replied. "Changes like these would typically take thousands of years to develop naturally."

Harding gave a whistle of amazement.

McKenna moved to another image showing the digestive tract, her finger tracing along unusual formations that caught the light from the monitor. "There's something else here that doesn't fit standard macaque biology."

"What am I looking at?" Harding asked, leaning closer.

"These partially digested materials," McKenna said, zooming in on grainy clusters nestled among the more recognizable food matter. "The composition is... unusual. Not typical forage for this species."

Vivian joined them at the screen, her expression shifting from professional interest to growing concern as she studied the image. "The cellular structure looks almost like—"

"Fungi," McKenna finished. "But not any standard variety documented in their natural diet."

Harding straightened, skepticism evident in the furrow of his brow. "You're suggesting what, exactly?"

McKenna hesitated, aware of how it would sound. Scientific training demanded caution with extraordinary claims, but the evidence before her pointed toward something they needed to address directly.

"I need to run a comprehensive analysis on the stomach contents, but based on preliminary observation, I believe we're seeing evidence of specific fungal matter with potential neurological effects."

"You're saying the monkeys are eating mushrooms that are making them *smarter*?" Harding's voice carried the disbelief of a practical man confronted with something outside his frame of reference. "Sounds like science fiction, Doc."

Vivian stepped in, her tone measured and precise. "It's not as far-fetched as it might seem, Sheriff. The relationship between certain compounds and neural development has been documented in multiple studies." She pulled up a reference document on her tablet, scrolling to highlight a particular section.

Several mycological compounds have demonstrated the capacity to promote neurogenesis—essentially, the growth of new brain cells and neural connections. There's precedent in both traditional ethnobotanical practices and modern pharmacological research."

McKenna nodded, grateful for Vivian's support. "If these macaques have discovered such compounds in the local ecosystem and have been consuming them regularly over multiple generations..." She let the implication sit.

"The effects could be cumulative," Vivian continued, warming to the scientific puzzle despite its alarming context. "Especially if they've developed cultural practices around consumption—teaching offspring which fungi to select, optimal quantities, specific timing."

Harding ran a hand over his face, processing this information against the backdrop of increasing incidents across town. "So we've got monkeys getting high on brain-boosting mushrooms and organizing strikes?"

"It's more complex than that," McKenna corrected gently. "These wouldn't be hallucinogenic in the recreational sense. Think of it more as a neural stimulant or enhancer, potentially affecting areas of the brain associated with problem-solving, pattern recognition, and social coordination. But..."

She pulled up comparison images showing normal macaque cerebral development beside their specimen's enhanced structure. "Combined with the abnormal brain development we're seeing, plus whatever environmental factors might be at play, we could be witnessing an unprecedented acceleration of cognitive evolution."

The three of them stood in silence for a moment, the implications settling like a wet blanket upon the room. Whatever they were facing wasn't just unusual animal behavior—it was potentially something entirely new entering their world.

"I need to conduct a comprehensive chemical analysis," McKenna said finally. "And we should collect environmental samples from the preserve, particularly areas where we've documented frequent macaque activity."

"This still feels like a stretch," Harding said, though his tone had shifted from outright skepticism to cautious consideration. "But it explains more than anything else we've got right now." He checked his watch. "How long will this analysis take?"

"Several hours for preliminary results," McKenna replied. "Longer for thorough identification of all compounds involved."

"Time we may not have," Vivian noted, nodding toward the window where emergency lights flashed in the distance. "If these cognitive enhancements are as significant as they seem, we need to understand what we're dealing with quickly."

Sheriff Harding straightened, decision made. "Start your analysis. I'll coordinate with Animal Control to collect environmental samples from the macaque territories."

As he turned to leave, McKenna called after him. "Sheriff? I'd advise putting extra patrols near the hardware store and auto parts shop tonight. Based on the pattern of items being taken, those would be logical targets."

Harding paused at the doorway, a hint of amusement crossing his features. "You really think these monkeys are planning their next heist?"

"Better safe than sorry," McKenna said firmly.

After Harding left, McKenna and Vivian began the internal examination. They worked methodically, documenting each step with photographs and recorded observations. The deeper they delved, the more McKenna's concerns were confirmed.

"The muscle fiber structure is unusually dense," Vivian noted as they examined tissue samples under the microscope. "Almost human-like in composition."

"And look at the liver," McKenna added. "The enzyme profile suggests adaptation to processing complex compounds—quite possibly psychoactive ones."

The brain examination proved most revealing. As they carefully removed and weighed the organ, both veterinarians exchanged concerned glances.

"Twenty-three percent heavier than standard for the species," McKenna recorded. "With pronounced development in the prefrontal cortex."

"We should preserve tissue samples for more detailed analysis," Vivian suggested. "This goes beyond my area of expertise."

"We need a primatologist," McKenna agreed. "Someone who specializes in cognitive development in non-human primates."

It was nearly midnight when they finished documenting their findings. McKenna stored tissue samples in the clinic's refrigeration unit while Vivian cleaned the examination area. Both women were exhausted but too uneasy about their discoveries to feel sleepy.

"What do you think it means?" Vivian asked as they prepared to leave. "These changes, the coordinated behavior..."

McKenna considered the question. "I think the Cypress Grove macaques have been evolving in ways we haven't noticed. The question is whether Earl shooting one of them will disrupt their normal patterns or..."

"Or what?"

"Or provoke some type of response." McKenna locked the clinic's back door, suddenly aware of how quiet the night had become. No insects chirping, no distant traffic—just eerie silence.

"Get some rest," she told Vivian. "Tomorrow I'll reach out to some university contacts, see if we can get a primate specialist to consult."

The drive home through Cypress Grove's darkened streets felt unusually tense. It was humid, even for the spring, and had begun to rain. The rhythmic sweep of her windshield wipers was the only sound breaking the oppressive silence. No frogs calling from the drainage ditches. No night insects buzzing around the streetlamps. Even the usual ambient hum of distant traffic vanished, as though the town had been wrapped in an unnatural shroud.

McKenna was scanning rooftops and trees, half-expecting to see the glint of baleful, watching eyes. Her headlights were dimmer than usual, barely penetrating the darkness that felt thicker, more substantial than ordinary night. The town square was deserted, the streetlights casting pools of sickly yellow illumination on empty benches where tourists photographed the friendly local macaques.

As she turned onto her street, McKenna's headlights swept across something small darting between houses—a fleeting specter. She slowed, heart suddenly hammering against her ribs, and peered into the darkness. Whatever it was had disappeared, but she couldn't shake the sense that it had recognized her vehicle, had deliberately shown itself before melting into the shadows. She pulled into her driveway with a sense of relief that evaporated as soon as she cut the engine. In the sudden hush, she could hear scratching—faint but unmistakable—coming from somewhere along the side of her house.

McKenna grabbed her phone, switching on its flashlight as she eased out of the truck. The rain had dwindled to a misty drizzle that clung to her hair and skin. She swept the beam across her front yard, shadows dancing between the azalea bushes and the sprawling octopus tree that dominated her property.

The scratching sound paused at her movement, then resumed—more deliberate now, rhythmic. It came from around the side of the house near the kitchen window.

"Hello? Kira, is that you?" she called out, immediately regretting breaking the silence.

She crept along the edge of the house, back pressed against the damp siding. Water dripped from the gutters, creating a soft percussion that nearly masked the scratching. She rounded the corner, light beam slicing through darkness.

Nothing. Just her garbage bins, garden hose coiled neatly on its hook, and the trellis of Carolina jasmine climbing toward her second-story window.

The scratching had stopped.

She approached the kitchen window, examining the sill and frame. Thin, parallel marks marred the paint—four distinct lines grouped together like... fingers. Or claws. Too deliberate to be random damage, too precise to be accidental.

She glanced up at the surrounding trees, suddenly sure she was being watched.

Feeling like a little girl afraid of the dark, she scuttled quickly to her front porch and, using her key, let herself in. The house felt like a sanctuary as she locked the door behind her. She found herself checking window latches twice, drawing curtains that normally remained open, peering between blinds at the darkened yard. Every shadow pulsed with potential threat. Every creak of the damp, settling house sent alarm bells ringing through her nervous system.

Downstairs secured, she moved quietly upstairs, pausing outside her daughter's room where music played softly.

"Kira?" she knocked gently. "I'm home."

The music volume lowered slightly. "Okay," came the flat response.

"Have you heard any noises, like scratching?"

"Nope."

McKenna sighed. It was probably just branches, or raccoons. "How was Dad?" she asked through the door.

A pause. "Fine. He's working with some anti-poaching unit now. Showed me pictures of elephants missing their tusks."

McKenna nodded to herself. Martin had always been good at sharing the exciting parts of his life, less adept at asking about his daughter's. "Good night, then. Love you."

Another pause, longer this time. "Night, Mom."

McKenna retreated to her bedroom, too tired to eat the dinner she'd missed. As she prepared for bed, her phone chimed with a text message. The number was unfamiliar, but the area code matched Cypress Grove's region.

*This is Earl Simmons. Sheriff gave me your number. The monkeys are back. Smashed all my trash cans. Weird sounds outside. What should I do?*

McKenna stared at the message, a chill slithering through her. She typed back: *Stay inside. Keep doors and windows locked. Call 911 if they try to enter your house. I'll come by first thing tomorrow.*

She hesitated, then added: *Don't shoot any more of them!*

Sleep proved elusive. McKenna lay awake, replaying the day's events in her mind. The marking system on Earl's shed. The markings on her window. The macaques observing from rooftops. The anatomical anomalies in the specimen they'd examined. The animal's purposeful diet. Each element odd on its own; together, they suggested something unprecedented. Every time she began to drift off, her mind conjured images of small, dexterous hands manipulating tools, of shrewd eyes glittering from darkness, of teeth bared in something too calculated to be called a snarl.

Shortly after three in the morning, her phone chimed again.

*They're taking things from my truck now. Hear tools being moved. Sheriff sent Dep. Miller but the bastards scrammed. Coming back now. Making clicking noises to each other. Different than normal monkey sounds.*

McKenna sat up, fully awake, her skin suddenly clammy despite the sultry night. The night around her felt alive, attentive. *Whatever happens, stay inside,* she typed back, her fingers trembling slightly on the screen.

Another message arrived almost immediately. *One of them is looking at me through the window. The big one with the bad eye. It knows I'm watching it watching me.*

McKenna read with widening eyes as another text from Earl came through:

*It SMILED at me.*

Outside McKenna's window, an owl hooted—then abruptly fell silent, the truncated call hanging in the mist like a severed thread. In the stillness that followed, she heard something moving across her roof. Small, careful steps. Deliberate. Precise. The soft scraping of what might be claws or might be tools testing different sections of the shingles, as though searching for structural weaknesses. The barely audible whisper of communication—not random chittering but patterned, intentional sounds and clicks passed between multiple entities.

Then, worst of all, a subtle scratching at her bedroom window—so faint she might have imagined it if not for the tiny squeak of something hard drawing a deliberate line across the glass.

McKenna lay frozen, afraid to look, more afraid not to. When she finally turned toward the sound, she caught only a glimpse—five small fingers splayed against the glass, gone so quickly she might have imagined them. But the condensation outline remained, slowly fading like an accusation.

Not random. Not afraid.

Scouting.

*Learning.*

# CHAPTER 3

McKenna woke with a start, her neck stiff from falling asleep upright against her headboard. The clock read 5:47 AM—dawn just breaking outside her window. After Earl's unsettling texts, she'd spent the remainder of the night alternating between watching the roof, checking on Kira, and dozing fitfully, a powerful flashlight and her old softball bat within arm's reach.

She stood, stretching muscles tight with tension, and moved to the window. The morning light revealed her yard empty and peaceful, birds beginning their usual chorus. Whatever had traversed her roof during the night was gone. Yet the memory of those deliberate footsteps remained vivid.

After a quick shower, she checked on Kira, finding her daughter still deeply asleep, one arm flung dramatically across her face in a pose reminiscent of her childhood. Downstairs, she made coffee and checked her phone. Five missed calls—three from Earl Simmons, one from Sheriff Harding, and one from the clinic. A string of text messages documented Earl's increasingly panicked night, culminating in a 4:30 AM message: *They're gone now. Deputies came again. Found my truck hood open, battery cables cut.*

McKenna had just finished responding to Earl when her phone rang. Vivian's name flashed on the screen. "Morning," she answered, pouring coffee into a travel mug, and adding a touch of milk. "I'm going to head to Earl's first, then come to the clinic."

"You might want to cancel that plan," Vivian replied, her voice coiled with unease. "The clinic's been broken into."

McKenna froze. "How bad?"

"Nothing stolen or damaged, surprisingly. But there are those marks—like the ones you said were on Earl's shed—scratched into the back door and the cabinets in Exam Room 3. Where we did the autopsy," she added pointedly.

"They knew which room we used."

"There's more. The tissue samples we took from the macaque—they're gone. The refrigeration unit was opened cleanly, nothing else disturbed."

McKenna set down her mug, mind racing. "I'm coming now. Have you called Harding?"

"He's already been here. Said to tell you he's headed to Earl's place next, then calling an emergency meeting at town hall at noon."

"I'll see you in fifteen minutes." McKenna ended the call and quickly texted Kira, explaining the situation and asking her to stay home. She added: *Keep doors and windows locked. Call me if you see ANY monkeys near the house.*

\* \* \*

The morning light had fully asserted itself as McKenna drove toward town, the distinctive Florida humidity already building. Her truck's radio crackled with local station WGRC, where the morning host was mid-sentence in what sounded like an unusually serious broadcast.

"—unprecedented number of reports overnight. The sheriff's Department confirms at least eighteen separate incidents involving the local macaque population. We're asking listeners to call in with their experiences while we wait for official word from Mayor Holden's office. Remember, these monkeys have been part of our community for decades without—oh, we have a caller from Palmetto Street. Ma'am, you say the monkeys took something from your garage?"

McKenna turned up the volume as an elderly woman's wavering voice filled the cab.

"Every garden tool I own. Pruning shears, loppers, my good Japanese digging knife. My late husband's toolbox—untouched for fifteen years, I tell you—completely emptied. But here's the weird part—they stacked my ceramic flowerpots by size before they left. Perfect circles. Like they were... I don't know... measuring or something."

The host sounded both doubtful and disturbed. "And you actually *saw* the macaques doing this?"

"Young man, I've been birdwatching for fifty years. I know how to observe without being seen. They worked in teams—lookouts, carriers, what seemed to be, um, a supervisor directing the whole operation. I saw what I saw!"

McKenna changed lanes to pass a slow-moving pickup pulling a horse trailer, her attention split between the road and the broadcast. More callers reported similar experiences: seemingly systematic thefts, always of tools or potential weapons, often with strange arrangements left behind—stones in geometric patterns, cords tied in complex knots, scratched markings on wood and metal surfaces.

By the time she reached the clinic, McKenna's concern had deepened into full-blown alarm. The parking lot contained two sheriff's department vehicles, Vivian's sedan, Marjorie's minivan, and one other vehicle. Marjorie stood outside the front entrance, directing a confused elderly man with a cat carrier back toward his car.

"We're closed today, Mr. Peterson! Emergency! Dr. Santos will call to reschedule!" Marjorie spotted McKenna pulling in and hurried over, her silver bob disheveled in a way McKenna had never seen before. "Thank goodness you're here. They keep coming—patients ignoring the closed sign, reporters asking questions, and now those protestors are setting up across the street."

McKenna followed Marjorie's gesture to where a small group was gathering on the public sidewalk opposite the clinic. A young man with a neatly trimmed beard was directing others in positioning signs bearing slogans like "PROTECT DON'T PERSECUTE" and "RESPECT ANIMAL RIGHTS."

"Who are they?" McKenna asked, grabbing her bag from the passenger seat.

"Call themselves 'Natural Balance.' Environmental group from Jacksonville. That one in charge—Justin Reeves—was on the morning news talking about the 'unwarranted persecution of an established primate community.'" Marjorie's air quotes conveyed her opinion of this characterization. "It was too funny, though—he kept calling them 'ma-ca-kays.'"

McKenna chuckled. "Muh-kak, rhymes with attack."

Marjorie shuddered. "Yeah, that's actually scary."

Inside, the clinic presented a troubling tableau. Deputy Miller was photographing a series of marks scratched into the cabinet doors of Examination Room 3—the same pattern McKenna had seen before, only larger and more precisely executed. Vivian stood in the corner, directing another deputy through the inventory of missing samples.

"They took the brain and liver tissues," Vivian reported as McKenna entered.

"They got everything?" McKenna asked.

"Not everything. And they couldn't get into the cooler, so the body is still here," Vivian replied.

McKenna examined the markings on the cabinets, noting the increased complexity compared to those at Earl's. "They're evolving their communication system. This is more elaborate than what I saw yesterday."

Deputy Miller looked up from his camera. "You really think the monkeys are leaving messages for us? Not just random damage?"

"Does this look random to you?" she traced the pattern without touching it—three vertical lines intersected by two horizontal ones, now surrounded by a series of smaller marks arranged in what appeared to be a deliberate sequence. "This is structured information. And targeting specific tissue samples shows a sort of... I don't know... focused intent."

Her phone rang—Sheriff Harding.

"I'm at Earl's place," he said without preamble. "You need to see this."

Fifteen minutes later, McKenna pulled up to Earl's property, where three patrol cars and Harding's personal truck created an impromptu barrier around the shed. Earl himself sat on his front porch steps, a shotgun across his bony knees despite the deputy standing guard nearby. His face was haggard, eyes bloodshot from his sleepless night.

"They came back at dawn," he said as McKenna approached. "Dozens of them. Moving like... like soldiers."

Harding emerged from the shed, his expression grim. The "Shock the Monkey" t-shirt had been replaced by his official uniform, complete with the starred badge of his office. "Doc," he acknowledged McKenna with a nod. "Looks like your primate pals have been busy."

McKenna batted away the myriad of gnats that hung in the thick, sultry air and peered inside the shed. The interior stopped McKenna in her tracks. Every tool had been removed from the walls. Storage bins had been emptied, their contents carefully sorted into piles in the center of the floor—screws with screws, nails with nails, each size group separate from the others. Most confounding were the walls themselves, now covered in elaborate scratched patterns—expanding on the basic design she had seen yesterday, developing into what looked like a crude map of Earl's property and the surrounding area.

"They mapped the place," she whispered, tracing the patterns with her eyes. "Look—this matches the tree line behind the property. And these marks correspond to the positions of the patrol cars yesterday."

Harding studied the inscriptions with narrowed eyes. "You're saying they created surveillance records?"

"And operational plans," McKenna indicated another section where lines suggested movement patterns converging on specific points. "This looks like they were planning their routes in."

Earl appeared in the doorway, ignoring the deputy's attempt to keep him back. "Told you they were organizing. Been telling people for months something ain't right with those apes. Nobody listened."

Harding turned to McKenna. "You mentioned you wanted to consult a primate specialist. Any luck with that?"

"I had a quick call with a former colleague from the research facility that serviced the zoo where I worked—Dr. Elijah Jackson. He's a cognitive primatologist specializing in non-human intelligence. If anyone can make sense of this behavior, it's him."

"Good. If he gets here in time, have him meet us at the town hall meeting. Mayor Holden's expanded it—mandatory attendance for business owners and emergency personnel." Harding checked his watch. "Ninety minutes from now."

McKenna spent the intervening time documenting the markings at Earl's shed, then stopping by three other residences where similar break-ins had occurred. She had her tranquilizer pistol holstered on her hip, just in case. At each location, she found the same pattern: the taking of tools and potential weapons, meticulous organization of remaining items, and marking systems carved into surfaces. The exactness and coordination evident in each site painted a puzzling picture of something far beyond normal animal behavior, no matter how smart they might be.

At one point, in the arboraceous, unfenced backyard of the Beaumont family, she detected a subtle shift in the surroundings and redirected her focus to the encircling woodland. The longer she stared into the foliage, the quieter it became. But when she sighed and turned to go back, the intermittent movement between trees resumed, more purposeful now. Figures were advancing, their shadows nearly indistinguishable from the dusky bark—visible mainly through their motion rather than form. Bewildered, she put her hand on her pistol and eased it out. She assumed a defensive stance, nearly kneeling as she surveyed the area. The limited range of her weapon—barely effective beyond thirty feet—left her feeling vulnerable. She maintained her aim, prepared for any sudden approach. An unsettling sensation of being surrounded took hold as more calculated movements flickered between the trunks. Whatever they were doing, there was no doubt the macaques were strategically closing distance while remaining sheltered by the forest.

The standoff stretched for minutes, sweat beading along McKenna's hairline as she maintained her position. The macaques suddenly, inexplicably, stopped advancing, maintaining their distance just beyond the effective range of her dart gun. Their eyes—several pairs—glinted from between leaves and branches, assessing and patient.

A rustle to her left drew her attention. A larger male had separated slightly from the group, his silvered face marked with a distinctive scar across his muzzle. Unlike the others, he made no attempt to conceal himself, standing fully exposed on a low-hanging branch. His posture wasn't threatening—if anything, he was studying her with the same studied detachment she might use when observing a new animal species.

McKenna kept her breathing steady, dart pistol still raised. The primate tilted his head, then raised one hand, palm facing outward. The gesture was unmistakably human—a signal to stop or wait. Then, with deliberate movements, he touched his chest, extended his arm toward McKenna, and finally pointed back toward the forest.

"What the hell?" McKenna whispered to herself.

The macaque repeated the sequence: chest, McKenna, forest. Then, maintaining eye contact, he backed away into the foliage. One by one, the other monkeys followed, their retreat as synchronized as their advance had been. The forest grew still again, birds cautiously resuming their calls as the troop withdrew.

McKenna remained frozen for several beats, listening for any sound of their return. When she finally lowered her weapon, her arms ached from strain. She backed toward the Beaumont's yard, unwilling to turn her back on the tree line until she reached the gate.

"They weren't hunting me," she murmured, trying to process what she'd witnessed. "They were... communicating?"

At her truck, McKenna fumbled with her keys, hands still unsteady. Inside the cab, she locked the doors before starting the engine, a reflexive action that struck her as both necessary and absurd.

She pulled away from the curb, checking her mirrors frequently for any sign of pursuit. Her phone chimed with a text message from an unknown number: *Landed in Jacksonville. Got rental car. ETA 45 minutes. Where should I meet you? - Elijah*

McKenna glanced at the time. The town hall meeting would start soon, and she had information that couldn't wait. She typed a quick response: *Town Hall, Main Street. You won't believe what's happening.*

\* \* \*

By the time she arrived, the parking lot was full and residents were streaming toward the entrance. The crowd's mood vibrated with a mixture of confusion, fear, and skepticism—typical of Cypress Grove's response to any disruption of its carefully cultivated small-town charm.

Inside, the main chamber had been arranged for maximum capacity, mismatched folding chairs filling the space usually reserved for more modest council meetings. Near the front, McKenna spotted Vivian saving her a seat. On the elevated platform at the front, Mayor Patricia Holden conferred with Sheriff Harding and two town council members, her pastel blue skirt suit and rigid bun lending her an air of structured composure.

"Any word from Dr. Jackson?" Vivian asked as McKenna took her seat.

"He's driving down now," McKenna replied. "Should be here within the hour."

Mayor Holden approached the microphone, tapping it twice before speaking in her practiced public-relations voice. "Ladies and gentlemen, thank you for assembling on such short notice. As many of you have heard, we've experienced a series of incidents involving our local macaque population. I want to assure everyone that the situation is under control and being addressed by the appropriate authorities."

A murmur of disagreement rippled through the crowd.

Earl Simmons, seated near the back, called out, "Under control? They screwed with my truck! Stole every tool I own!"

Mayor Holden's smile tightened. "Mr. Simmons, we'll have time for individual reports shortly. Sheriff Harding will now brief us on the official assessment of the situation."

Harding took the microphone, his imposing stature and direct manner providing a striking contrast to the Mayor's polished evasiveness. "Since yesterday afternoon, we've documented several separate incidents involving the macaque colony. The pattern shows coordinated entry to properties, targeted theft of specific items—mainly tools, cutting implements, wiring, and mechanical components—and evidence of some kind of exchange of ideas between groups through marking systems."

He gestured toward a deputy who activated a projector, displaying photographs of the various symbols and etchings found around town. "These have been found at every incident site, increasing in sophistication over time. What began as simple territorial markers appears to be evolving into a more polished system."

"Are you seriously suggesting the monkeys are writing to each other?" called a skeptical voice from the audience.

Some people tittered.

"I'm reporting what we've observed," Harding replied evenly. "The evidence suggests coordinated activity beyond normal macaque behavior. Dr. McKenna Dubrow has done a preliminary exam of one specimen and consulted with a primatology expert who's en route to Cypress Grove now."

Mayor Holden quickly reclaimed the microphone. "While we investigate these unusual occurrences, I want to emphasize the importance of maintaining Cypress Grove's reputation as a safe, welcoming tourist destination. The macaques have been a beloved attraction for decades, and we must avoid overreaction that could damage our community's primary economic driver."

A hand shot up from the middle of the audience. "What about the attack on Mrs. Abernathy this morning? Would you call that an overreaction?"

The crowd stirred, multiple voices joining in with questions and reports of stolen items, a missing pet, and strange sightings. Mayor Holden attempted to restore order, her composure slipping as the volume increased.

The sheriff stepped forward again. "We have three reported incidents of direct aggression toward residents. All were minor scratches and one bite that didn't break skin, but they do suggest a deviation from their usual behavior patterns. We're implementing a temporary curfew from sunset to sunrise and advising residents to secure homes and businesses."

As the meeting continued, McKenna felt a tap on her shoulder. A tall, well-groomed man in his mid-thirties stood in the aisle, his expression both serious and somehow amused. Despite having flown and driven, Dr. Elijah Jackson looked impeccable in dark jeans and a crisp button-down shirt, his short afro perfectly shaped, his nails—as McKenna had expected—immaculately maintained.

"McKenna," he greeted her with a firm handshake. "Sounds like you've got quite the simian situation here."

"You could say that. Thank you for coming so quickly." She introduced him to Vivian, and they shook hands.

"I've brought some equipment to examine your specimen," Elijah said. "And I'd like to review those marking systems in person. The photos you sent are fascinating—evidence of symbolic thinking well beyond documented capabilities for *Macaca fascicularis*."

Their conversation was interrupted by a commotion at the chamber entrance.

The protestors McKenna had seen outside her clinic were pushing their way in, led by Justin Reeves, whose confident stride and raised voice commanded attention despite his relatively short stature. He carried a megaphone and was followed by about fifteen supporters bearing signs defending the macaques.

"The people of Cypress Grove need to hear the truth!" Justin announced through the speaker as he marched toward the front of the chamber. "These intelligent primates are responding to threats against their community! The shooting of an innocent macaque—" he mangled the word again—"has provoked a natural defensive response!"

Mayor Holden looked torn between maintaining order and avoiding a confrontation that might make the evening news. "Sir, we welcome all viewpoints, but there's a procedure for addressing the council—"

"Procedures won't protect defenseless monkeys from trigger-happy residents and overreaching authorities," Justin interrupted, positioning himself at the side of the platform. "Natural Balance has documented the systematic harassment of non-human primates throughout Florida. What's happening in Cypress Grove is the inevitable result of encroachment on their territory and careless disruption of their social structures."

McKenna felt her patience evaporating. She stood, addressing Justin directly. "I've examined one of the macaques." She slowly pronounced the word correctly and saw, with some satisfaction, the man's cheeks redden. "Their behavior isn't a 'natural defensive response.' They're exhibiting coordinated, strategic actions with tool use far beyond normal capabilities. They've targeted specific equipment, disabled vehicles, and are using a developing communication system to coordinate actions across multiple groups."

Justin turned toward her, his expression dismissive. "And *you* are?"

"Dr. McKenna Dubrow. Veterinarian. Former researcher at the Primate Cognition Institute, and former Apex Predator Specialist at the Miami Zoo."

"Ah, another so-called expert who sees animals as specimens rather than sentient beings." Justin's condescension was palpable. He straightened his bespoke jean jacket, making sure that the Natural Balance logo on his t-shirt could be plainly seen. "Let me explain something to you, Dr. Dubrow. When an indigenous population—even a non-human one—is threatened, they adapt. These *macaques*," he said, mirroring her over-enunciation, "have lived here for generations. They've observed human behavior, learned from it. What you're calling 'unnatural' is simply their intelligence expressing itself in response to these egregious and deadly threats."

Before McKenna could respond, Elijah stepped forward. "Dr. Elijah Jackson, PhD., primatologist, University of Florida. While adaptive behavior is certainly within the capacity of *Macaca fascicularis*, the collection of tools, development of symbolic communication, and coordinated group actions described here represent a quantum leap beyond documented capabilities. This suggests either radical cognitive enhancement or outside influence."

Justin looked momentarily caught off-guard by Elijah's expertise, but quickly recovered. "The scientific establishment consistently underestimates non-human intelligence because it threatens human exceptionalism. These sentient beings deserve protection while we study their emerging capabilities, not extermination because they frighten us."

"No one has suggested extermination," McKenna countered, frustration edging her voice. "But we need to understand what's happening before someone gets seriously hurt—human or macaque."

Mayor Holden, seeing an opportunity to reclaim control of the meeting, stepped between them. "This is precisely the kind of thoughtful discussion we need. Sheriff Harding is implementing safety measures while the doctors investigate the scientific aspects. Natural Balance's concerns will be incorporated into our approach."

The diplomatic platitudes might have defused the situation if not for the sudden blaring of emergency tones from multiple phones throughout the chamber. The county's emergency alert system had activated, sending simultaneous notifications that cut through the mayor's speech.

Harding checked his phone, his expression darkening. He stepped to the microphone, interrupting the Mayor mid-sentence. "We have three attacks in progress. Riverside Retirement Community, Palmetto Street, and the east side shopping center. Multiple injuries reported."

The chamber erupted in chaos as people checked their phones and called family members. Through the confusion, McKenna heard snippets of information—macaque groups targeting elderly residents, deliberate disabling of security systems, theft of medications, and additional tools.

"We need to get to the clinic," McKenna told Vivian and Elijah as they pushed against the tide of people heading for the exits.

Outside, emergency sirens wailed as patrol cars and ambulances raced in different directions. In the distance, toward the eastern edge of town near the preserve, a thin column of smoke rose into the afternoon sky—evidence of a growing crisis. The ever-present gnats hovered in the air, and scrub jays squawked excitedly in the nearby cypress branches.

As they hurried toward their vehicles, McKenna caught sight of Justin Reeves directing his group to form a human chain across the street, blocking emergency vehicles from responding to the Riverside Retirement Community. His megaphone crackled as he shouted about "preserving the habitat" and "peaceful coexistence."

"Still think it's just adaptive behavior?" McKenna asked Elijah as they reached her truck.

His expression turned grave. "No... Whatever's happening here seems to go beyond adaptation. This is transformation—deliberate and purposeful. And if I'm right about what might be causing it, Cypress Grove has much bigger problems than tourism trouble."

As if to emphasize his point, a series of power transformers exploded across town, plunging entire blocks into darkness despite the early afternoon sun. In the trees surrounding the town hall parking lot, shapes moved with swift assuredness—small figures swinging from branch to branch, observing the human panic below with predatory eyes.

# CHAPTER 4

D r. Elijah Jackson had expected an interesting case study when he received McKenna Dubrow's call about anomalous macaque behavior. What he hadn't expected was to find himself navigating through chaos as he drove into the tiny borough of Cypress Grove. Emergency vehicles whooshed past his rented Land Cruiser, their sirens screaming. Residents hurried down sidewalks, casting nervous glances at trees and rooftops. Every telephone pole he passed bore freshly printed flyers warning about macaque encounters.

Small-town panic had a particular flavor, Elijah noted—equal parts legitimate concern and overblown hysteria. He'd seen it before in field research locations from Borneo to Costa Rica, whenever human and primate territories overlapped. Usually, the situation was a simple case of habituation gone wrong—wild primates becoming too comfortable around people, losing their natural fear, and causing minor property damage.

But what McKenna had described during their brief phone conversation suggested something far beyond habituation. Coordinated action. Tool use beyond documented capabilities. Symbolic communication. If even half of her observations were accurate, the Cypress Grove macaque colony represented something unprecedented in primatology.

Elijah tightened his grip on the steering wheel, excitement and scientific curiosity mingling beneath his careful professional demeanor. He'd built his career studying cognitive development in non-human primates, focusing specifically on how environmental pressures influenced problem-solving capabilities. His last paper—"Cognitive Leaps in Isolated Primate Populations: The Intersection of Genetic Drift and Environmental Challenge"—had been well-received but criticized for its speculative conclusions about accelerated evolution under specific conditions. If the Cypress Grove macaques truly were exhibiting the behaviors McKenna described, his theories might find dramatic vindication.

The town hall meeting had provided his first real glimpse of the situation—both the physical evidence in the photographs and the psychological impact on the community. McKenna's clinical observations aligned with his own theories about potential cognitive development, while the panicked reactions of residents and the misguided protectiveness of the activist group created a volatile social environment around what should be a carefully contained, well-managed scientific investigation.

Now, following McKenna's truck through neighborhoods showing increasing signs of macaque activity—broken windows, disturbed gardens, strange chickenscratch on exterior walls—Elijah mentally catalogued everything he observed. He wished he could pull over and take pictures, but there would be time enough for that later. His trained eye caught details others might miss: the consistent height of damage, suggesting standardized tool use rather than random destruction; the systematic nature of the breaches, targeting specific entry points rather than opportunistic ones; and most notably, the absence of typical macaque droppings or territorial markings.

These weren't animals behaving like animals. They were animals behaving like something else entirely.

McKenna pulled into the parking lot of her clinic, now cordoned off with yellow police tape. Elijah parked alongside her and gathered his equipment bag—specialized tools for primate research, including non-invasive cognitive testing apparatus, high-resolution cameras for behavioral documentation, and sample collection kits.

"Sheriff posted a deputy inside after the break-in," McKenna explained as they approached the building. Vivian parked and quickly fell into step with them. "But he had to leave during the attacks. We should secure the remaining specimens before examining the colony site."

Elijah nodded, studying the exterior of the converted bungalow. "The entry points show planning—note how they avoided breaking glass or causing obvious damage. They found the vulnerabilities in your security system."

"You talk about them like they're executing a military operation," Vivian remarked, unlocking the clinic's front door with a key code.

"Because they are, in their way," Elijah replied, following her inside. "Military strategy at its core is about resource acquisition, territory control, and neutralizing threats. If these macaques have experienced a cognitive leap, they're applying problem-solving to survival priorities."

The interior of the clinic showed signs of searching—drawers opened, cabinet doors ajar, items moved but not damaged. Elijah immediately noticed the marking system scratched into various surfaces, approaching one cabinet to examine the patterns more closely.

"Fascinating," he murmured, removing a digital microscope from his bag and connecting it to his tablet. "The depth and angle consistency suggests deliberate control rather than instinctive marking behavior. And the pattern repetition with variations indicates informational content—not unlike primitive writing systems."

"Can you interpret any of it?" McKenna asked, securing the remaining tissue samples in a portable cooling unit.

Elijah captured high-resolution images before responding. "Not yet, but pattern recognition software might help identify recurrent elements. What's most significant is that they're creating external memory storage—extending reasoning beyond individual recall. That's a fundamental cognitive milestone."

He continued examining the clinic while McKenna and Vivian gathered materials, finding additional evidence of the macaques' unusual behavior—organized arrangement of small objects, precisely placed handprints in dust.

The implications chilled Elijah to the marrow; that would mean the macaques had been this way for a long time and were now *choosing* to show off their skills. "We need to see the colony site," he said finally, straightening from his inspection of a lower cabinet. "Behavior emerges from environment. Whatever's happening with these macaques, the explanation will be in their habitat."

"I'm going to go home and check on my cats, if you don't mind," Vivian said, wringing her hands.

"Of course," McKenna replied. "Just keep your phone on, okay?"

* * *

Thirty minutes later, Elijah found himself trekking through the dense subtropical vegetation of the de facto preserve surrounding Cypress Grove. He moved with practiced efficiency through the undergrowth, his boots leaving minimal impressions on the damp ground.

Years of fieldwork had taught him how to navigate challenging terrain while remaining observant of his surroundings. McKenna followed close behind, showing a surprising comfort with the environment for someone whose primary work was clinical.

"The main colony has historically centered around the southeastern section," she explained as they navigated around a cypress knee. "About two miles in, near a spring-fed pool. The area's been informally designated as macaque territory for decades I've been told, though they've always foraged throughout the area."

Elijah nodded, mentally mapping their position relative to town. "Classic edge habitat exploitation. They maintain a natural home range while accessing human resources. It's a common pattern for populations living near human settlements." He paused, examining a broken branch showing signs of deliberate manipulation rather than natural breakage. "But this is different."

As they progressed deeper into the preserve, Elijah catalogued increasingly concerning evidence of organized activity. Natural materials had been gathered and modified—vines stripped and braided into stronger cordage, stones collected and arranged by size, plant matter sorted by apparent utility. Small structures appeared at regular intervals—platforms constructed in trees, connected by crude but effective bridges of woven branches.

"They've created a transportation infrastructure," he noted, photographing one such bridge. "Allowing rapid movement without ground exposure. Military strategy again—maintaining high ground advantage and invisible deployment capabilities."

McKenna pointed to a nearby tree where similar bridges converged. "That wasn't here three months ago when I treated a wounded deer in this area. None of this was."

"Accelerated development," Elijah agreed. "Far beyond normal rates of innovation."

The trail opened into a small clearing surrounding the spring-fed pool McKenna had mentioned. Under normal circumstances, this would have been the heart of macaque territory—a water source with surrounding fruiting trees providing ideal habitat. Instead, they found it completely abandoned.

Elijah knelt beside the water, examining disturbed mud showing a multitude of macaque footprints. "They've relocated recently. Within the last forty-eight hours, judging by print degradation." He moved methodically around the clearing, reconstructing activities through physical evidence. "They were gathering here in large numbers. See how the vegetation is trampled in concentric circles? Classic formation for group meetings."

At the far edge of the clearing, Elijah discovered something that stopped him mid-step. "McKenna. Look at this."

In a relatively flat area of mud, partially protected by overhanging foliage, a crude but recognizable representation of Cypress Grove had been created. The macaques had used sticks, stones, and mud to construct a three-dimensional map of the town, with key structures clearly identifiable—the town square, major roads, the veterinary clinic, the sheriff's Department, even the water tower on the north side. More concerning were the small markers placed at strategic locations throughout the model—colored stones and arranged twigs indicating what appeared to be targets or objectives.

"This is..." McKenna began, then fell silent as she processed what they were seeing.

"Tactical planning," Elijah finished for her, the scientist in him momentarily overcome by the implications. "They're actively strategizing."

"Huh," McKenna mumbled. "When I saw the markings at Earl's place and his neighbors', I was wondering if they were trying to communicate with us. But it doesn't seem that way now."

Elijah only nodded as he photographed the mud map from multiple angles, capturing every detail for later analysis. As he worked, his mind processed the evolutionary implications. Crab-eating macaques were already among the most intelligent non-ape primates, known for their problem-solving abilities and adaptation to human environments. Their neural architecture supported advanced cognition, with well-developed prefrontal cortices and complex social structures that encouraged information sharing.

But this level of organization suggested something more—a transformation that evolutionary timescales couldn't explain.

He remembered learning in high school about the Depression-era hobo code, a visual language wandering workers used to share tips and warnings with each other. Much like these macaques now—developing their simple dialect by adapting to their surroundings. Those chalk or charcoal marks across fences, buildings, and tree trunks served as useful graffiti, pointing the way to jobs, food, or danger.

"What could cause this degree of enhanced function?" McKenna asked, echoing his thoughts.

Elijah considered the possibilities, mentally reviewing research on cognitive development. "There are several potential mechanisms. Isolated populations sometimes experience accelerated evolution due to genetic drift and intense natural selection. It's called the founder effect—when a small group establishes a new population, any unusual traits become concentrated and magnified through subsequent generations."

He gestured to their surroundings. "These macaques have been isolated here for, what, forty, fifty years? That's about eight to ten generations. Under normal circumstances, not enough time for significant evolutionary change. But if the founding population already possessed unusual cognitive traits, and if environmental pressures selected for intelligence..."

"But this seems beyond even accelerated natural selection," McKenna pressed.

Elijah nodded, his scientific caution battling with the evident reality before them. "Which suggests external factors. You mentioned unusual physical development in the specimen you examined—enlarged cranial capacity, enhanced neural density. Those changes require either genetic modification or neurochemical intervention." He looked up from the mud map, meeting her eyes directly. "Has there ever been research conducted in this area? Military, pharmaceutical, anything using primates as test subjects?"

McKenna shook her head. "Not that I'm aware of. The colony was established when a movie crew abandoned them here in the late seventies. Before that..." she paused, considering. "I don't actually know their origin. The story around town just mentions a jungle movie that was filming nearby."

"We need to trace that history," Elijah said, returning to his documentation of the site. "Research facilities sometimes sold 'retired' test subjects to entertainment companies. If these macaques came from an experimental program..."

He trailed off as something caught his attention at the edge of the map. A small arrangement of sticks had been formed into a distinct shape—one that triggered recognition from his extensive knowledge of primate research history.

"That symbol," he said quietly, photographing it specifically. "It looks a lot like the logo of a discontinued neurological enhancement program from the Cold War era. Project APEX. They were working on creating enhanced battlefield awareness in primate models as a precursor to human applications."

"How do you know about that?" McKenna asked.

"My doctoral research included reviewing primate research programs that were later discontinued on ethical grounds. They were redacted, but I could still read a lot between the lines. Most were presumed terminated, their test subjects euthanized or put in sanctuaries." Elijah straightened, a shuddering chill making its way through him despite the humid air. "But now I'm not so sure. If these macaques are descendants of APEX subjects, with latent genetic modifications now expressing..."

A subtle sound interrupted his explanation—a barely perceptible rustling in the canopy above them. Elijah froze, his fieldwork instincts taking over. Without moving his head, he shifted his eyes upward, scanning the branches.

"We're being watched," he said, voice a whisper. "Don't make any sudden movements."

McKenna tensed but followed his lead, continuing to examine the mud map as if unaware of the scrutiny. "How many?" she breathed.

"At least a dozen that I can detect." Elijah continued his documentation, acting as if nothing had changed. "They're practicing perimeter security—maintaining surveillance while remaining concealed. Another military concept."

As they worked, Elijah surreptitiously tracked the watchers, noting their discipline and coordination. Unlike normal macaque behavior, which would include occasional vocalizations or movement betraying position, these observers maintained almost perfect stealth. Only the slightest shifting of weight on branches or momentary exposure through leaf gaps revealed their presence.

"We should continue as if we haven't noticed them," he advised. "Complete our documentation and leave without confrontation. They're assessing our intentions, not immediately threatening."

"I hope you're right," McKenna mumbled, placing her hand on the butt of her holstered tranquilizer gun.

For twenty more minutes, they thoroughly recorded the abandoned colony site, cataloguing evidence of organizational complexity and cognitive advancement. Throughout the process, the hidden onlookers remained, their discipline never wavering.

Elijah wasn't afraid exactly, but he was unnerved. Whether imagination or reality, he sensed a shift in the attention of their observers—a focusing of intent, an evaluation of his understanding.

"We should go," he said quietly to McKenna. "We've learned what we can for now. Any longer and we risk being perceived as a threat to their territory."

They retraced their steps through the preserve, Elijah maintaining awareness of their surroundings without betraying concern; while there was more to it, it was true that animals could smell fear.

The sensation of being followed persisted—not just by the original observers but by additional presences moving parallel to their path, tracking their retreat. Elijah could feel them—silent phantoms flitting through the canopy, maintaining perfect intervals between one another as they shadowed the humans' progress. Every few seconds, he caught glimpses of russet fur or the flash of bared teeth through the foliage. They weren't simply following out of curiosity as normal macaques might. This was an escort, a carefully orchestrated surveillance operation maintaining visual contact while communicating positions to one another through some imperceptible means.

A few macaques leapfrogged ahead to establish observation points, then allowed others to pass while they maintained their watch. Some traveled through the high branches while others kept to the lower understory, creating a three-dimensional net of awareness around the retreating scientists. What worried Elijah most wasn't their presence, but the calculated intent behind their movements—the unmistakable sense that these weren't merely animals acting on instinct, but beings executing a strategic plan with clear objectives and roles.

"They're ushering us out," he noted as they neared the preserve's edge. "Maintaining surveillance until we leave their territory."

"Is that normal macaque behavior?" McKenna asked.

"Nothing about this is normal," Elijah replied. "They're applying strategic concepts that require abstract thinking. Territory control, coordinated surveillance, and resource acquisition for future use rather than immediate need. These are advanced cognitive functions requiring frontal lobe development well beyond typical macaque capabilities."

As they emerged from the preserve onto the maintenance road where they'd left McKenna's truck, Elijah felt the watchful presences withdraw—not departing entirely but establishing a perimeter at the forest edge. He scanned the tree line, catching glimpses of small shapes moving with disciplined coordination.

"What now?" McKenna asked as they loaded their equipment.

Elijah considered their options, weighing scientific protocols against the escalating situation. "We need to analyze the data we've collected and establish a research baseline. Document the behavioral and physiological anomalies. Develop a hypothesis for the cognitive enhancement mechanism."

McKenna got in and started the truck, relieved to hear the intact rumble of the engine. She checked her phone as service returned. "Two more attacks reported while we were here. The sheriff has set up a command center at the high school. They're expecting us there."

"First the clinic," Elijah insisted, slamming the passenger door and fastening his seatbelt. "We need to secure our findings and check the specimen you mentioned. The physical evidence is crucial to understanding what we're dealing with."

The drive back to the clinic took them through neighborhoods showing increasing signs of disturbance—broken windows, damaged vehicles, residents hurriedly loading possessions into cars. The macaque situation was escalating from curiosity to crisis with dizzying speed.

Elijah processed what they'd discovered, mentally composing the research paper that this would eventually become, assuming they successfully navigated the immediate crisis. "*Unprecedented Cognitive Enhancement in Isolated Macaque Population: Evidence of Directed Evolution or External Intervention.*" The title would need work, but the findings would revolutionize understanding of primate cognitive potential.

The clinic appeared undisturbed as they pulled into the parking lot, the police tape still in place from earlier. His rental was there, and, as expected, Vivian's car was gone. Nothing externally indicated additional tampering or entry. Yet as they approached the front door, Elijah's skin prickled with instinctive alarm.

"Wait," he said as McKenna reached for the door. "Something's not right."

They examined the front door and saw that the security sensor had been repositioned fractionally, and the door hinges showed signs of careful manipulation.

"They've been here while we were gone," he concluded.

McKenna frowned, inputting her security code with heightened caution. The system disarmed with a confirmatory beep, seemingly normal. She pushed the door open slowly, revealing the reception area beyond, apparently untouched.

"Should we call the sheriff?" she asked.

Elijah considered the situation. "Let me check first. If they've been here, they've already left. Their pattern suggests information gathering rather than destruction."

He wondered just how many macaques there were. They'd seen several in the preserve, and, according to McKenna's text messages, many others had been spotted in town and the surrounding neighborhoods.

He moved methodically through the clinic, using his well-honed observational skills to detect subtle changes. The examination room where they'd studied the macaque specimen showed signs of thorough investigation—equipment minutely repositioned, cabinet contents examined and replaced.

Most significant was what they didn't find—additional damage, missing items, or threatening displays. This had been a precise reconnaissance operation, not a retaliatory attack.

"They're studying us as carefully as we're studying them," Elijah muttered, returning to the reception area where McKenna waited. "Learning our methods, our equipment, our capabilities."

"But they didn't take anything this time," she noted.

"They didn't need to." Elijah gestured around the clinic. "They've catalogued everything here, just as thoroughly as we documented their colony site. The next phase won't be about information gathering."

"What will it be about?" McKenna asked, the question hanging in the air between them.

Before Elijah could answer, his phone buzzed with an incoming message—a colleague from the university responding to his request for information about Project APEX. The attached historical document confirmed his suspicions, showing a research facility that had operated in North Florida during the 1970s, using crab-eating macaques for cognitive enhancement experiments involving both genetic modification and neurochemical interventions.

The facility's location was listed as ten miles northeast of where they now stood.

"McKenna," he said, showing her the document. "I think I know where your macaques came from." He met her eyes, the scientist in him both alarmed and fascinated by the implications.

"Yeah. The movie people. They brought them in from the Philippines."

"Maybe some of them... but not all of them. What we're seeing now is the fruition of something the APEX researchers were trying to create—primate intelligence with strategic capability. Living weapons."

"Oh, my god," McKenna said. "I need to get to my daughter."

The lights in the clinic flickered momentarily, as if in response to Elijah's warning.

Outside, the sun was beginning to set, casting long, sinuous shadows across the parking lot. In those shadows, Elijah caught a glimpse of movement—small, coordinated, purposeful.

# CHAPTER 5

McKenna snapped on a fresh pair of nitrile gloves as Vivian adjusted the overhead surgical light. Room 3 had been transformed into an impromptu research lab. Stainless steel instruments gleamed on a tray beside the table where the macaque's body was laid out.

They had four bodies to choose from now, a grim inventory of subjects that grew as frightened townspeople continued their relentless hunt. Armed with shotguns and hunting rifles, the local vigilantes tracked the macaques through woods and backyards, shooting them on sight with brutal disregard. They left the bullet-riddled corpses where they fell—in drainage ditches, tangled in garden fences, sprawled across the switchgrass—making no effort to dispose of or study what they clearly viewed as vermin. McKenna couldn't help but note the irony that these violent deaths, motivated by fear and ignorance, were providing the very specimens she needed for her scientific investigation.

"Recording's active," Vivian announced, checking the camera mounted on a tripod in the corner. "Audio and visual documentation initiated at 7:34 PM, Monday, April 28th."

McKenna glanced at Elijah, who stood opposite her across the examination table, his own gloves already in place. Despite the grim circumstances, she noted a familiar gleam of scientific curiosity in his eyes—the same intensity she remembered from their days as colleagues at the Primate Cognition Institute. She'd left that world behind when experimental protocols began prioritizing medical applications over animal welfare, but Elijah had remained, walking the delicate line between advancing knowledge and maintaining ethical standards.

McKenna's hands moved mechanically through the initial examination, her mind drifting back to the Miami Zoo—her sanctuary after fleeing the compromises of her research. The tropical mists delivered by machine, the vibrant manmade foliage, the sounds of exotic birds amplified through the zoo's speakers. It had felt like starting over.

Then came Martin, the charismatic veterinary director with his passionate conservation speeches and tender hands. Their romance unfolded amid medical rounds and fundraising galas. His proposal in the butterfly garden. Their small wedding by the flamingo pond.

When Kira arrived, McKenna remembered how Martin had cradled their daughter while McKenna watched, heart full to bursting. They'd created their own little ecosystem of love and purpose.

Until Kenya. Until Sophia.

Four years ago, and the words still burned. "I never meant for this to happen," he'd said, suitcases already packed. The mammologist had offered him fieldwork with elephants—his dream—and apparently, a connection McKenna—or even their daughter—couldn't compete with.

"I'll always love Kira," he'd promised.

But weekly calls became monthly. Postcards with elephants replaced visits. And McKenna learned to be both parents while rebuilding her shattered world.

She blinked back to the present, aware of Elijah watching her with quiet concern.

"We'll begin with an external examination before proceeding to cranial and thoracic cavities," McKenna said, focusing on the task at hand. "Dr. Jackson will document observations while Dr. Santos and I perform the dissection."

Elijah nodded, tablet at the ready. "I'll correlate physical findings with behavioral observations and Project APEX protocols, if applicable."

McKenna took a deep breath, centering herself. This wasn't a standard veterinary procedure or even a typical wildlife necropsy. This examination might reveal the key to understanding the unprecedented situation unfolding outside their walls—the transformation of a tourist attraction into an organized threat.

"Subject is a male *Macaca fascicularis*, approximately nine years old based on dentition," she began, moving methodically. "Cause of death was shotgun trauma, with extensive damage to thoracic and abdominal cavities. Spinal cord severed."

She carefully examined areas unaffected by the gunshot damage, noting abnormalities as she found them. "Musculature shows unusual development, particularly in the upper limbs and hands."

As she worked, McKenna found herself slipping back into research protocols she had abandoned years ago, the precise language and meticulous observation coming back like muscle memory. Each finding built upon the last, creating a picture of something far beyond normal macaque physiology.

"Proceeding to cranial examination," she announced after they had documented the external features. She selected a bone saw from the instrument tray, its weight familiar in her hand.

"Before you open the cranium," Elijah interjected, "there's a specific feature I'd like to examine." He indicated a point at the base of the skull. "The APEX documentation mentioned development of an accessory neural bundle connecting the cerebellum to higher processing centers. It would manifest as a slight protrusion here."

McKenna adjusted her approach, feeling the area Elijah indicated. A slight bulge was indeed present where the skull met the first cervical vertebra. "Noted. Abnormal formation present at the atlanto-occipital junction. Approximately seven millimeters in diameter."

She proceeded with the cranial opening, carefully cutting along the predetermined path to remove the cap of the skull, revealing the brain beneath. The room fell silent as all three doctors stared at the exposed organ.

Vivian spoke, breaking the silence. "The brain mass is dramatically oversized for the species. Maybe even bigger than the first one..."

"Thirty percent larger than documented standards," Elijah confirmed, consulting reference data on his tablet. "With pronounced development in the prefrontal cortex and unusual convolution patterns in the parietal regions."

McKenna carefully removed the brain, placing it in a weighed container. "Confirmed. Brain mass is 107 grams, well beyond the standard range of 65-85 grams for adult male *Macaca fascicularis*. Not unlike what we saw on the one Earl shot."

The implications were left stranded in the air as they proceeded. This wasn't subtle variation or even pronounced adaptation. This was a fundamental restructuring of neural architecture, something that would typically require thousands of generations of evolutionary pressure—or deliberate intervention.

The thoracic examination revealed less dramatic but equally significant abnormalities—enhanced pulmonary capacity, cardiovascular adaptations suggesting improved oxygen utilization, and unusual liver enzyme profiles indicating adaptation to processing complex compounds.

It was the digestive system, however, that yielded the most surprising evidence. McKenna carefully extracted partially digested material from the intestinal tract, placing samples on slides for microscopic examination.

"Vivian, can you identify these plant structures?" she asked, stepping back from the microscope after her initial observation.

Vivian leaned in, adjusting the focus slightly. "Some components are typical forest floor vegetation, fruits—standard macaque diet. But there's something else..." She manipulated the slide, isolating unusual cellular structures. "This appears to be a fungal species. Possible psilocybe genus, but with unusual structural adaptations."

"Is it the same as the mushrooms we saw in the first autopsy?" McKenna asked.

Elijah quickly joined them at the microscope, his expression intensifying as he viewed the specimen. "Not just any psilocybe. This resembles a compound classified under APEX protocols—a synthetic hybrid created to enhance neural plasticity in test subjects. They called it Compound P-17." He straightened, meeting McKenna's eyes. "It was shelved—supposedly—after subjects began showing unpredictable leaps of thought, reasoning, and cooperative behavior that researchers couldn't control."

"You're saying what—that these macaques are consuming descendants of an experimental cognitive enhancer?" McKenna asked, struggling to maintain scientific detachment.

"It's a plausible mechanism for the accelerated development we're seeing," Elijah confirmed. "If the original research subjects escaped with knowledge of the compound, and if it established itself in the local ecosystem..." He gestured to the brain still resting in its container. "Combined with already enhanced neural architecture from the original experiments, regular consumption of such a compound could produce exactly the kind of cognitive evolutionary jump we're witnessing."

McKenna's reply was interrupted by a faint sound from somewhere in the clinic—a light but insistent scratching against the exterior wall. All three froze, listening intently as the sound dragged slowly across the surface like nails on a chalkboard.

"Could be branches in the wind," Vivian suggested, but the tremor in her voice betrayed what they all knew: nothing natural moved with such deliberate precision.

The scratching stopped. Silence hung heavy for three heartbeats. Then it came again—not just from one location but from everywhere at once—the north wall, the roof access, the rear door. A synchronized symphony of scrapes and taps, as though the entire building was being methodically tested for weaknesses. Mapped. Studied.

"They're here," Elijah whispered, shrinking from the windows as shadows flickered past the blinds. "Multiple points of approach. Coordinated reconnaissance."

McKenna's mouth went dry. The clinic's walls, once a sanctuary of science and healing, now felt paper-thin. Her mind raced through their options, each worse than the last. The security system was basic, designed to deter human break-ins—not an organized assault by creatures that could navigate spaces humans couldn't reach.

"Vivian, call Sheriff Harding," she managed, her voice unusually high. "Elijah, help me secure these samples."

The scratching intensified, now interspersed with a rhythmic metallic tapping—tools being systematically tested against windows, vents, door frames. Tap-tap-tap. Pause. Scrape-scrape. The sounds came faster, more insistent, punctuated by soft, guttural vocalizations unlike anything McKenna had ever heard from a macaque—not random chitters but patterned, almost linguistic exchanges. Commands. Reports. Planning.

Her hands shook as she organized tissue samples into containers, the plastic rattling against the counter. Sweat trickled down her spine despite the room's air-conditioned chill.

"No signal," Vivian hissed, the screen of her phone casting a sickly blue glow across her face. "Not just weak—completely blocked. They must be jamming the service somehow."

"The landline," McKenna said, already moving toward reception.

Before she could reach the door, the lights stuttered—once, twice—then died with a finality that sucked all the oxygen from the room. For three terrible seconds, they stood in perfect darkness, hearing nothing but their own ragged breathing and the soft, anticipatory rustling outside.

The emergency lighting sputtered to life, bathing everything in a sickly red glow that transformed familiar equipment into grotesque, threatening shapes. Shadows stretched and distorted across the walls, some moving independently of any visible source.

"They've cut the power," Elijah observed, but McKenna could hear his academic detachment crumbling around the edges. "Tactical standard—disrupt communication and visibility before entry."

"Oh, shit," McKenna breathed, her own clinical vocabulary deserting her entirely.

The scrabbling sounds intensified—a multitude of small bodies moving across the roof, down the walls, around every possible entrance. The walls seemed to crawl with unseen presences. The air grew heavy with a musky, animal scent seeping through the ventilation system.

A sudden crash shattered the tension—glass breaking in the reception area, followed by the patter of small feet on tile. Not the chaotic scrambling of frightened animals, but the measured cadence of coordinated movement. Through the examination room's interior window, McKenna glimpsed shapes slithering through the darkness—silhouettes too purposeful to be anything but an invasion force.

"Barricade the door," she gasped, already heaving the equipment cabinet across the floor. It screeched against tile, obscenely loud in the confined space. Vivian and Elijah threw their weight behind the metal supply cart, pushing it against the door just as something heavy slammed into it from the other side.

The impact vibrated through McKenna's bones. The door shuddered in its frame. Through its small window, she caught fragmented glimpses of the attackers—a reflective eye catching the emergency light, yellowed fangs bared in a snarl, small, sinewy hands gripping tools with dexterity.

The pounding intensified, the door buckling under methodical assault. From somewhere above, ceiling tiles shifted. Plaster dust rained down. McKenna felt the noose tightening—they were surrounded, cornered like prey.

"They're after the specimens," Elijah said, breathless as he turned to gather crucial samples. "Same as before—removing evidence of their adaptations."

The thought struck McKenna with cold certainty: that's not all they want. The primitive parts of her brain recognized the smell of focused aggression, of calculated violence. These creatures wanted retribution. Blood. *Their* blood.

A ceiling tile crashed down in a shower of dust and insulation. McKenna caught a flash of movement—something slight and dark plummeting into the room with terrifying accuracy. Before she could react, two more followed, landing in different corners like commandos deploying from helicopters.

The emergency lights cast their forms in hellish red, transforming familiar macaque features into something from a nightmare. They moved with fluid, predatory grace, muscles rippling under fur slick with rain or sweat... or blood. Their eyes—horribly, unmistakably intelligent—cataloged everything in the room, marking exits, threats, objectives.

McKenna recognized the leader instantly. In the crimson glow, his damaged eye gleamed like a pearl submerged in blood. His scar tissue pulled his face into a permanent leer that exposed yellowed canines.

He studied them with an almost philosophical detachment before making a series of sharp, staccato sounds—not animal noises but those precise commands again. His subordinates responded instantly, one moving toward the specimen while another approached their documentation equipment.

"They're not showing aggression, just purpose," Elijah whispered, maintaining eye contact with Alpha as though hypnotized by a cobra.

McKenna begged to differ. She watched in horror as the macaques collected brain tissue samples with acuity, their thin fingers manipulating instruments designed for human hands. The third took hold of the digital camera, then methodically crushed the device under a metal paperweight.

"I'm not letting them take everything," McKenna breathed, slowly reaching toward a duplicate sample hidden in the cooling unit under the counter.

Alpha's head snapped toward her, tracking the movement with unwavering focus. The scarred tissue around his evil eye twitched. He made a sharp gesture—a command too clear to misinterpret.

One of his subordinates materialized at McKenna's side with preternatural speed. The scalpel in its hand caught the red light, the edge gleaming. It held the blade with the confidence of a surgeon—or an assassin.

"McKenna, don't," Vivian pleaded, frozen as another macaque focused on her with sinister concentration. "They understand intent."

Alpha looked deliberately at the scalpel's razor edge, then directly into McKenna's eyes. His lips peeled back in what might have been a smile in a human face but resembled nothing so much as a death mask on his. His good eye glinted with something McKenna's brain refused to process—a calculated malevolence that transcended species.

The door hinges gave way with a screech of protesting metal. The barricade toppled inward, nearly crushing Viv. Through the gap poured a flood of dark shapes—at least a dozen more macaques swarming into the room like a colony of ants consuming prey. The stench of wet fur, musk, and something McKenna's hindbrain identified as rage filled the confined space.

They moved with exactitude, some securing exits while others collected items with practiced efficiency—tissue samples, documentation, surgical instruments. Their breathing filled the room with a soft, collective hiss, punctuated by the clicks and chirps of their abbreviated communication.

The most troubling sight came last. Two larger macaques carefully wrapped their fallen friend's body in the examination drape, their fingers working with agility to secure precise knots. With ceremonial care, they lifted the shrouded form between them.

"They're honoring their dead while securing operational security," Elijah marveled. "That's..."

"Human," McKenna finished, the word sticking in her throat like a stone.

Human, maybe, but that wasn't necessarily good or benevolent. Humans were the most depraved, vicious animals of all—and these creatures had learned from the masters.

Amid the chaos, two macaques broke away from the group. They moved toward the back of the clinic, their instincts driving them toward the cooler where the remaining bodies lay in wait. The soft thud of their feet against the tile barely registered above the fray.

With deft fingers, one pried open the cooler door while the other stood guard, scanning for threats. The cold air rushed out, mingling with the warm scent of panic that clung to McKenna and her team. Inside, the bodies remained untouched, each one a potential key to understanding more about their kind's sudden evolution.

The first macaque hesitated only a moment before gripping a limp limb and dragging it toward the door. The second followed suit, grasping another corpse with surprising gentleness as it maneuvered around discarded instruments.

Alpha observed from his perch, eyes glinting with satisfaction. It seemed he understood the importance of keeping these specimens away from human hands—knowledge they couldn't allow to be dissected or weaponized.

For one heart-stopping moment, the dominant male turned to face McKenna directly. Their eyes locked across the chaos—not veterinarian and animal, but commanders on opposite sides of an emerging war. Recognition passed between them, a tacit acknowledgment that boundaries had been irrevocably crossed.

Alpha's lips once again pulled back in a grotesque approximation of a human smile, the expression all the more unnerving for its deliberate mimicry. He issued a series of sharp, precise commands, and his forces began their withdrawal with the same chilling coordination with which they had entered.

They departed like smoke through windows, vents, and ceiling access points, carrying away the evidence of their true nature.

Within minutes, the invasion force had vanished, leaving behind only the stench of their presence and the wreckage of scientific inquiry. The premeditated violence of their visit floated in the air like a promise—this was merely the opening move in a longer game.

McKenna, Vivian, and Elijah stood frozen in the aftermath, the red emergency lights casting their shocked faces in the same infernal glow that had transformed the macaques into creatures of horror. The examination table lay empty, stripped of its secrets. Sample containers gaped open like tiny coffins. Only Elijah's tablet, clutched against his chest throughout the encounter, remained intact.

"Well," Vivian finally said, her steady tone stretched thin over barely contained hysteria, "I think we can definitively say these aren't normal macaques."

"Yeah, and I think we just failed their ethics committee review," McKenna said, her voice hollow with exhausted terror. "Turns out when you dissect a monkey's uncle, they take it personally. Wonder if they'll publish a paper on human defensive behaviors in captivity."

Her companions were still too shaken even to crack a halfhearted grin at the gallows humor.

"They're protecting operational security," Elijah said, his academic vocabulary a fragile shield against the horror they'd witnessed. "Removing evidence of their physiological adaptations. Standard protocol for any intelligence operation when compromised."

In the distance, sirens wailed—human reinforcements arriving far too late. McKenna knew with cold certainty that the crucial evidence was already gone, carried away by small, strong hands with disturbing dexterity. Hands that could hold tools. Build things. Destroy things. Kill things.

"We still have the data I transferred," Elijah said, holding up his tablet like a talisman against the darkness. "And the fungal samples they missed." He indicated a small container that had fallen behind a cabinet during the assault. "It's not much, but it's something."

Sheriff Harding's imposing figure appeared in the doorway moments later, weapon drawn, deputies fanning out behind him to secure the violated space. His expression shifted from readiness to stunned disbelief as he surveyed the scene.

But McKenna barely noticed his arrival. She was still locked in the memory of Alpha's calculated smile, the eerie promise in his undamaged eye. The macaques hadn't just taken their evidence—they'd issued a declaration. And in the red-tinged darkness of the ruined clinic, she knew with certainty that none of them were prepared for what was coming.

"What the hell happened here?" the sheriff demanded, holstering his gun after confirming the immediate threat had passed.

"They took back their dead," McKenna replied solemnly. "And made sure we couldn't prove what they've become."

Harding's skepticism from earlier had vanished, replaced by the grim acceptance of a law enforcement officer confronting an unprecedented threat. "Tell me what we're dealing with, Doc. No scientific qualifications, no maybes. What are these things?"

McKenna exchanged glances with Elijah, who nodded slightly, encouraging her to voice what they now understood. She took a deep breath, formulating her response with care.

"They're not just ordinary monkeys anymore, Sheriff. They're the result of old military experiments that have been passed down through generations, made even stronger by special plants they've found in the swamp. They can think like humans in certain ways—as we've seen, they can plan ahead strategically, they use tools with purpose, and they've developed their own system of symbols to communicate with each other."

She paused, the full implications settling heavily on her shoulders. "And they're organized for a fight. I think what we're facing isn't animal defensive behavior. It's warfare."

The sheriff absorbed this assessment, his expression hardening as he processed its implications for Cypress Grove. "Can they be reasoned with? Negotiated with?"

"Unknown," Elijah interjected. "They clearly understand human intentions and can anticipate actions. Whether that extends to complex communication or diplomatic concepts..." He shrugged. "We simply don't have enough data."

"What we do know," McKenna added, "is that they're adapting fast, learning from each encounter. The longer we wait to develop a response, the more sophisticated they will become."

Harding nodded grimly, already reaching for his radio to call in additional resources. "I've established a command center at the high school gym. Mayor Holden's there with the town council and emergency services. We need you three there immediately to brief everyone."

As they gathered what little evidence remained and prepared to leave the ransacked clinic, McKenna found her gaze drawn to a small, shiny object on the floor near the exit. She bent to retrieve it—a polished stone, unnaturally smooth, with divots etched into its surface.

"They left this deliberately," Elijah noted, examining the stone without touching it. "It's a message."

"What does it say?" Vivian asked.

Elijah carefully photographed the stone from multiple angles before allowing McKenna to place it in an evidence bag. "I have no idea. But the fact that they're attempting to communicate rather than simply attack might be a good sign."

As they followed Sheriff Harding to the small armada of police vehicles, emergency lights painting the darkened street in pulses of red and blue, she found herself wondering what other evidence the macaques might have left behind—and what messages those artifacts might contain.

But first, they needed to survive the night. And across Cypress Grove, lights were going out one by one as methodical, organized raiding parties of macaques continued their operations under the cover of darkness.

# CHAPTER 6

E arl Simmons was well into his third beer of the evening when he heard the scratching.

"Goddamn apes," he muttered, setting the can on his cluttered coffee table with enough force to splash foam onto last Sunday's fishing news. "Oh, excuse me," he said louder, rolling his eyes. "Monkeys."

Three days since he'd shot that monkey at his shed. Three days of sleepless nights and jumping at shadows. A young deputy, still wet behind the ears, had taken his statement about being watched, but he could tell by her sideways glance that she thought he was just a trigger-happy redneck. Only that veterinarian woman seemed to take him seriously.

Earl heaved himself up from his sagging recliner, wincing at the twinge in his lower back, a souvenir of twenty years hauling lumber at the mill before it shut down. He shuffled to the kitchen window, flicking on the porch light that illuminated his scrubby yard.

Nothing moved in the sickly yellow glow—just his rusted-out pickup, the row of garbage cans he'd secured with bungee cords, and the tool shed where he'd caught that monkey trying to steal his pruning shears. Everything looked normal, but Earl knew better. He'd been hunting since he was eight years old. He knew when he was being watched.

The scratching came again, this time from the opposite side of the house.

Earl moved to his gun cabinet—a battered oak relic inherited from his father—and unlocked it with hands that weren't quite steady. He withdrew his Remington 870, the same shotgun he'd used on that monkey. The familiar weight provided some comfort as he began loading shells into it.

*They're just animals*, he told himself. *Just smart little thieves, nothing more.*

But his hands betrayed his thoughts, trembling more as he loaded the fourth shell, then a fifth. The memory of that monkey's eyes as it died haunted him—not the glazed emptiness of death, but the moment before, when understanding had flickered there. Recognition of what was happening. *Judgment.*

Earl didn't consider himself a superstitious man, but he'd grown up in rural Florida, had heard all the old tales. His grandmother had warned him about killing certain animals—how they'd send their kin after you, how they'd remember a face. She'd told him that crows held grudges. He'd always laughed at such nonsense.

He wasn't laughing now.

The porch light flickered, then went out.

"Shit and double-damn," Earl muttered, moving to the front window. The darkness outside was thicker somehow, more substantial. He peered into it, trying to make out shapes in his yard, when a flash of movement at the edge of his vision made him jerk back.

Something small had darted past the window—too fast to identify, but he knew. The hair on the back of his neck stood up.

Earl moved methodically through his double-wide, checking locks on doors and windows. He'd installed new deadbolts after the second night, had reinforced the window frames with additional screws. His home wasn't exactly Fort Knox, but it would keep out animals. Even smart ones.

At the back door, he paused. The scratching had stopped, replaced by something worse—silence. Not the natural quiet of a Florida night, with its chorus of insects and distant highway sounds, but a vacuum of noise that felt deliberately imposed. As if everything in a half-mile radius was holding its breath.

He positioned himself in the living room, shotgun at the ready, back to the wall where he could see both the front door and the hallway leading to the rear entrance. His phone lay on the coffee table—Sheriff Harding's number already dialed, his thumb hovering over the call button.

*They're just monkeys*, he told himself again. *I'm a grown man with a shotgun.*

A sharp crack from the bathroom window shattered his self-admonishment.

"Hello?" Earl called out, immediately cursing himself for the stupidity of it. What did he expect, a response? "I've got a gun!" he added, with more bravado than he felt.

The silence stretched, elastic and unnatural.

Then came the sound he'd been dreading—not breaking glass or splintering wood, but the soft, deliberate click of his back door latch disengaging. He'd locked it; he was sure he'd locked it. Yet the metallic snick was unmistakable.

Earl raised the weapon, aiming it down the darkened hallway, finger tensing on the trigger. "I'll shoot!" he shouted, his voice sounding thin and reedy in his own ears.

Nothing moved in the darkness. No sound came from the back of the house.

Earl fumbled for the light switch with his left hand, keeping the shotgun trained on the hallway. The overhead fixture remained dark when he flicked it. He tried again. Nothing. The little bastards had cut his power.

His heart hammered against his ribs, a caged animal desperate for escape. With an unsteady hand, he reached for his phone, pressing the call button for Sheriff Harding. The screen flashed briefly, then went dark. No service.

The night outside pressed against the windows like a living thing, peering in, measuring his fear. Taking stock of him. Earl backed toward the kitchen, where he kept a flashlight in the drawer beside the sink. He needed light. Needed to see what he was facing.

His heel caught on something—the edge of the area rug—and he stumbled slightly. It was only a tiny misstep, a momentary loss of balance, but it was enough.

They were waiting for exactly such an opportunity.

From the shadows of the hallway erupted a small, dark shape, moving with alarming speed. Earl fired instinctively, the shotgun's roar deafening in the small space. The blast tore a chunk from his wall, missing the darting figure completely.

Before he could pump another shell into the chamber, a second shape launched itself from beneath his coffee table—a hiding place he'd never thought to check. It struck his leg with unexpected weight, small but powerful hands gripping his calf, sharp teeth sinking into the meat of his thigh.

Earl screamed, more from shock than pain, and tried to swing the shotgun downward. A third macaque dropped from somewhere above—the ceiling crawlspace, he realized—landing on his shoulder like a circus acrobat. Its weight and momentum threw him off-balance, sending him staggering against the wall. He managed to shrug it off, its claws swiping his neck as it leapt away. He fired again, wildly, blasting a hole in his ceiling. Plaster dust rained down, stinging his eyes.

The macaque on his leg released its bite and sprang away, but not before Earl felt something warm and wet spreading down his jeans. Blood. His blood.

He tried to steady himself, to locate his attackers in the darkness, but they seemed to be everywhere and nowhere—flitting shadows just at the periphery of his vision. Moving with an uncanny coordination that should have been impossible. Communicating without sound.

"Get out of my house!" Earl bellowed, rage momentarily overcoming his fear. He pumped the shotgun again, swinging it in a wide arc before him.

There was a flicker of movement to his right. Earl pivoted and fired, rewarded this time by a shriek and the wet thump of a small, furry body hitting the wall. One down.

His momentary triumph evaporated as something heavy struck the back of his knee, collapsing his leg under him. Earl went down hard, the shotgun clattering away across the worn wooden floor.

He lunged for it, fingers stretching, brushing the warm barrel. Then weight landed on his back—not just one macaque but at least three, coordinating their attack with horrifying accuracy. Strong hands gripped his hair, yanking his head back with a force that brought tears to his eyes.

Earl bucked and writhed, trying to dislodge them, but they clung with the tenacity of their species, their strength disproportionate to their size. He felt hot breath against his ear, the unmistakable stink of animal musk.

With a desperate heave, he managed to roll onto his side, dislodging two of the creatures. He scrambled to his knees, then to his feet, staggering toward the front door. If he could just get outside, to his truck...

He made it three steps before something tangled between his ankles—a trap, he realized with dawning horror, deliberately set while they'd distracted him. Fishing line, probably from his own tackle box. Earl pitched forward, arms windmilling uselessly, crashing to the floor with enough force to drive the breath from his lungs.

For a moment, he lay stunned, unable to move, unable to process the calculated nature of what was happening to him. Pain radiated from his chest where he'd hit the floor, black spots dancing at the edges of his vision as his lungs struggled to refill. The realization that these creatures had deliberately set a trap—had anticipated his movements and prepared for them—sent an icy wave of terror washing through him that paralyzed him more effectively than the fall itself. This wasn't random aggression; this was planned. His mind rebelled against the implications, against everything he thought he knew about the natural world. The macaques weren't just reacting—they were thinking, strategizing, executing with military precision that shouldn't exist in the animal kingdom.

Rolling onto his back, Earl found himself face to face with a large male macaque perched on his coffee table. Even in the dimness, he recognized the distinctive cloudy eye and puckered scar that marked its face. He'd seen it watching from the trees after he'd shot the one at his shed. Had seen its awful, unnatural understanding.

The macaque tilted its head, studying Earl with an intelligence that surpassed species. Its damaged eye caught what little light there was, reflecting it back like a malevolent owl. Slowly, deliberately, it raised one hand, displaying something that made Earl's stomach clench—his cell phone, screen glowing faintly.

With precision that boggled the mind, the macaque's thumb moved across the screen, navigating to his recent calls. Finding Sheriff Harding's number. Then, with a glance at Earl that could only be described as contemptuous, it dropped the phone and brought one foot down with calculated force.

The screen shattered with a sound like breaking ice on a winter pond.

Earl tried to crawl backward, to put distance between himself and this devil, but the other macaques had positioned themselves behind him. He felt small hands gripping his ankles, his belt, his shirt—not attacking, but holding him in place. For what, he didn't want to know.

"Please," he whispered, the word foreign on his tongue. Earl Simmons had never begged for anything in his life. "Please don't."

The scarred macaque—Alpha, though Earl had no way of knowing this name—made a sound deep in its throat. Not normal monkey chatter, but something modulated and complex. A signal.

The hands released him.

For one wild, hopeful moment, Earl thought they were letting him go. He scrambled to his feet, heart pounding, eyes darting toward the shotgun still lying near the wall. Too far. The door, then.

He managed two steps before they were on him again—not restraining this time, but harrying, like wolves circling wounded prey. One darted in to slash at his calf, then sprang away. Another leapt onto his back briefly, pulling his hair and raking claws across his scalp before leaping off.

Earl staggered under a new onslaught, his mind reeling as he struggled to keep his bearings amidst the chaos. Assaults rained down from every angle, a blur of fur and flashing teeth, and he couldn't tell where the next strike would come from. His vision was marred by crimson tendrils seeping into his eyes from the gash on his scalp, the sting of the wound mingling with the warm, sticky flow. His thigh pulsated with a deep, persistent ache where the macaques' teeth had clamped down with brutal force.

With each step, pain lanced through him, stabs of the savage reality he now faced. Earl's breaths came in ragged gasps, the taste of copper on his tongue as he vainly tried to clear his sight. The room spun around him, the familiar surroundings of his trailer now a twisted arena, the scene of a macabre dance orchestrated by vicious animals. The sounds of his own labored breathing and the soft, menacing rustle of movement around him were all that broke the silence.

Earl's hands, slick with sweat and blood, trembled at his sides. His body, though battered, operated on sheer adrenaline, the primal instinct for survival now overriding the pain. He stumbled, his legs threatening to give out, but the will to live kept him upright, fueled by the terror of what would happen if he fell.

The macaques, with their quick, darting movements, anticipated his every move, as if they could sense his despair, his faltering resolve.

In the midst of this nightmarish assault, Earl's mind raced, frantically searching for a way out, a glimmer of hope amidst the overwhelming dread. But every potential escape was met with the reality of his situation—surrounded, outnumbered, and at the mercy of creatures driven by an intelligence that was all too apparent now.

With immense effort, Earl tried to focus, to push past the fear and pain. He knew he had to act, to do something—anything—to change the course of this grim situation. But as he cast a wild glance around the room, the sight of the macaques, their eyes gleaming with an otherworldly intensity, only served to underscore the hopelessness of his plight. And then, amidst the sea of malevolent faces, he caught

sight of the shotgun, still agonizingly out of reach, its very presence
a cruel jeer.

Earl's heart, already pounding like a drum in his chest, skipped a
beat as a new wave of fear sluiced over him. He could feel the macaques
closing in, their movements precise and purposeful under the leader's
watchful glare. The scarred macaque remained an ominous figure atop
the coffee table, its silence more terrifying than any sound, its control
over its troop absolute.

With one final, desperate surge of energy, Earl lunged toward the
shotgun, his fingers outstretched, yearning for the solid, reassuring
touch of steel. But as he did, a fresh agony seared through his leg, and
he felt the grip of the macaques tighten on his body, their small hands
unyielding as they dragged him back into the fray.

They were toying with him, he realized with nauseating clarity.
Playing with him like cats with a mouse. Letting him think escape was
possible before dashing that hope. Making it last.

"I'm sorry," he gasped, not even sure what he was apologizing for.
For shooting one of them? For existing in their territory? For being
human? "I'm sorry!"

Alpha watched from its perch, unmoving amid the choreographed
chaos. Its role was not to participate but to direct—the conductor of
this cruel, grotesque symphony.

Earl made a final, desperate lunge for the shotgun. His fingers had
just closed around the barrel when he felt small but incredibly powerful hands on his shoulders, his arms, his legs—not harrying now but
restraining with purpose.

He twisted his head to see the big monkey approaching with considered steps. In its hand gleamed something metallic that caught
the faint moonlight filtering through the window—his fishing knife,
taken from the tackle box they'd somehow opened.

Earl's throat worked, trying to form words, prayers, curses—anything to forestall what was coming. But no sound emerged beyond a choked whimper.

Alpha's face showed nothing as it raised the knife—no anger, no triumph, not even the satisfaction of revenge. Just calculated purpose, a task to be completed. Its marred eye caught the blade's gleam as it brought the knife toward Earl's exposed throat.

The last thing Earl saw was his own terrified reflection in that milky orb, distorted but recognizable. A human made small and helpless by something he'd considered beneath him. Something he'd underestimated.

Something that had evolved beyond his comprehension.

The knife descended like the blade on a guillotine, and Earl's world dissolved into hot, wet darkness.

Alpha stood over the body as blood pooled on the cheap wood-vinyl, spreading in a perfect semicircle around Earl's head. The other macaques maintained their positions, neither celebrating their victory nor showing revulsion at its aftermath. They simply waited for the next command.

With unhurried calm, Alpha wiped the knife clean on Earl's shirt, then placed it carefully beside the body—not discarded but positioned with specific intent. A message. Evidence not just of killing but of understanding the significance of how and why it was done.

Then, with a series of short, precise vocalizations, he directed the group to begin the next phase of their operation. They moved through Earl's home with methodical proficiency, gathering specific items—tools, weapons, communication devices—while leaving others untouched.

Before departing, Alpha paused at the door, looking back at what remained of his adversary. The simian face remained expressionless, its eyes reflecting nothing now. This hadn't been mere revenge—it had been tactical necessity. Elimination of a demonstrated threat.

The first of many such necessities to come.

As the macaques melted into the darkness outside, the Florida night reclaimed its voice—insects resuming their chorus, frogs calling from nearby ditches, a distant big rig passing on the highway. Normal sounds returning to fill the vacuum they had temporarily imposed.

But for Earl Simmons, the silence would last forever.

# CHAPTER 7

The Cypress Grove High School gymnasium had been transformed overnight into a makeshift command center. Folding tables lined the polished wooden floor where basketball games had been played just days earlier. Maps of the town and surrounding preserve covered the walls, with red pins marking confirmed macaque incidents. Sheriff Harding had established a dispatch station near the bleachers, where deputies and animal control officers coordinated with volunteer spotters via radio. The constant crackle of transmissions underscored the gravity of their situation.

McKenna sat at a table in the corner where she, Elijah, and Vivian had spent the night reconstructing their autopsy findings, mostly from memory. Coffee cups and energy drink cans littered the surface, evidence of their sleepless efforts. Elijah's tablet displayed their compiled notes, a fraction of what they had originally documented.

"Brain mass approximately 107 grams," McKenna recited into the recording app, rubbing her eyes. "Frontal lobe development exceeded standard parameters by roughly thirty percent, with unusual neural density in areas associated with planning and spatial reasoning."

Vivian nodded, adding her own recollections. "Liver enzymes showed adaptation to processing complex compounds, suggesting regular exposure to psychoactive substances. The fungal matter in the digestive tract resembled psilocybe varieties but with structural distinctions consistent with genetic modification."

"Project APEX documentation references similar compounds," Elijah confirmed, pulling up the historical files he'd acquired through his university contacts. "The program focused on enhancing battle-field awareness and decision-making in primate models before human trials. Experimental subjects demonstrated accelerated pattern recognition and unprecedented cooperative behavior."

McKenna frowned, something still bothering her about the fungal samples. "But the original program was ended decades ago. How would the compounds survive in the elements all this time?"

"Self-propagation," Elijah suggested. "If the fungal species was engineered for resilience, it could have established itself in the preserve ecosystem. The macaques must have discovered its effects and deliberately cultivated it."

"Farming psychedelics," Vivian said with a hint of her counterpart's dark humor. "Monkey see, monkey do agriculture."

"More worrying is the possibility of intentional consumption management," Elijah continued. "Not just consumption but controlled dosing—targeting developing young and pregnant females to accelerate cognitive development in subsequent generations."

McKenna was about to respond when the gymnasium doors burst open, admitting Sheriff Harding and Mayor Holden, both looking remarkably put-together despite the crisis. The mayor's blue skirt suit remained crisp, her tight bun impeccable, though the absence of her usual glasses gave her a slightly unfocused appearance. Beside her, the sheriff's uniform conveyed authority and preparedness, his expression set in hardline determination.

"Listen up," Harding called, his voice cutting through the background chatter. "We've established a town-wide alert system and protection protocols. Each neighborhood has a designated safe house equipped with emergency supplies. Deputy Miller is distributing information packets with safety guidelines."

Mayor Holden stepped forward, her practiced smile strained at the edges. "We've contacted state wildlife authorities for assistance. Until they arrive, we're implementing precautionary measures while maintaining essential services. Grocery stores and the medical clinic will remain open, with security personnel on site. All other businesses are advised to close temporarily."

McKenna watched the faces of her neighbors and fellow townspeople as they absorbed these announcements. The skepticism that had pervaded yesterday's town hall meeting had vanished, replaced by anxious resolve. Nothing united a community like a common threat, she thought.

"Dr. Dubrow," Harding called, motioning her forward. "Please brief everyone on what you've learned about these monkeys and how to protect themselves."

McKenna moved to the center of the gym, acutely aware of the expectant faces turned toward her. Behind her, Elijah and Vivian gathered their notes, ready to provide support.

"Based on our examination of one specimen and observation of their behavior, we're dealing with macaques that have undergone significant cognitive enhancement," she began, her voice steady despite her exhaustion. "They demonstrate strategic thinking, tool use, and coordinated action beyond normal capabilities for their species. Their physical adaptations include enhanced brain development, particularly in areas associated with planning and problem-solving."

"In English, Doc!" a sullen male voice called out. She sighed. *Dumb it down*. "Based on what we've seen from the dead monkey and watching how they behave, these aren't normal macaques. They can think ahead, use tools, and work together in ways regular monkeys simply can't. Their brains are physically different too—especially in the parts that handle planning and solving problems."

Murmurs rippled through the crowd as she continued, outlining the macaques' observed tactics and potential weaknesses.

"How do we stop them?" called someone from the back.

"Regular safety measures probably won't work," McKenna said honestly. "They've figured out our security systems and know how to get around them. Your best defense is to stay in groups—they've been avoiding confronting multiple adults together. Lock up all your tools, especially anything sharp, and keep in touch with your neighbors."

As she stepped back, Deputy Miller began distributing bright orange flyers with safety guidelines.

Her phone vibrated—a text from Kira. *Town's going crazy. School canceled. Everyone's talking about monkey attacks. Are you OK?*

McKenna had spent a frantic hour at dawn confirming her daughter's safety after the clinic attack. Kira had been surprisingly cooperative, agreeing to stay with Marjorie rather than alone at their house near the preserve edge. McKenna quickly replied: *Still at command center. Stay with Marjorie. DO NOT go outside alone no matter what. I'll update when I can. Love you.*

The gymnasium doors opened again, admitting Justin Reeves and his Natural Balance group, now expanded to over twenty protesters. They carried different signs today: COEXISTENCE NOT EX-TERMINATION and RESPECT MACAQUE INTELLIGENCE.

Justin strode purposefully toward Mayor Holden, his expression self-righteous and cocky.

"Mayor Holden, Natural Balance demands representation in these proceedings," he announced loudly. "These macaques are demonstrating unprecedented cognitive capabilities that warrant protection and study, not deadly force."

The mayor's lips curved into a polite smile. "Mr. Reeves, we welcome all perspectives. However, after multiple property invasions and injuries to residents, our primary concern must be public safety."

"The macaques are simply responding to human aggression with logical defensive measures," Justin explained with an exaggerated patience, as if speaking to children. "If we'd just listen to the experts—like *those of us* who've studied animal behavior—we could establish protected zones and non-interference protocols. Then they'd have absolutely no reason to continue these actions. It's really quite simple ecology if you'd bother to understand it instead of immediately resorting to violence like typical small-town thinkers."

McKenna had reached her limit. Sleep deprivation and the memory of Alpha's calculating gaze broke through her professional restraint. She approached Justin, positioning herself directly in his line of sight.

"You don't understand what we're dealing with," she said, keeping her voice low but intense. "These aren't normal macaques responding to territorial threats. They've undergone cognitive enhancement through both genetic modification and environmental factors. They're demonstrating military-style strategic thinking and organized campaign planning."

Justin's dismissive expression only deepened her frustration. "You don't know what you're talking about here," he replied. "You just want to justify control and exploitation."

"Did you not hear about the clinic attack?" McKenna pressed.

"All consistent with adaptive responses to perceived threats," Justin countered smoothly. "Your clinic conducted an autopsy on one of their community members. They recognized your actions as threatening and responded accordingly."

Before she could respond, a commotion erupted near the dispatch station. A volunteer spotter had arrived, breathless and wide-eyed. "Fires in the preserve," he reported. "At least six locations around the town perimeter. They started all at once about ten minutes ago."

Harding immediately moved to the wall map, where the spotter indicated the fire locations. "Miller, coordinate with fire services. Direct them to prioritize residential areas near the edge of the preserve. Crosby, assemble the eastern neighborhood watch teams."

As the command center shifted into higher alert, Elijah joined McKenna, studying the map with interest. "Strategic fire placement," he noted quietly. "They're creating a perimeter control system—smoke to reduce visibility, directed flame patterns to channel movement along specific routes. Classic containment tactics."

"You sound almost admiring," McKenna observed.

A hint of Elijah's old snark surfaced. "Professionally, I have to appreciate the cognitive leap this represents. Personally, I'm hoping Smokey the Bear shows up."

She chuckled, thinking back to their camaraderie as colleagues with off-kilter senses of humor.

Their conversation was interrupted by the arrival of a tall, weathered man with silver at his temples, dressed in camouflage hunting gear with a rifle slung over his shoulder. His expression said he meant business.

Darren Cooper moved with the quiet confidence of someone accustomed to tracking and hunting through wilderness. His deeply etched scowl intensified as he approached Sheriff Harding.

"Sheriff," he acknowledged gruffly. "Checked the western preserve approach like you asked. Found evidence of orderly movement—multiple trails, deliberately obscured but trackable with the right eyes. They're using the drainage culverts to access the town without being spotted."

"Can you block the access points?" Harding asked.

Cooper shook his head. "Not without heavy equipment. And they've established alternative routes—they're thinking ahead, setting up contingencies."

"Mr. Cooper has volunteered to help track macaque movements," Harding explained to McKenna, Vivian, and Elijah. "He knows the preserve better than anyone in Cypress Grove."

"I know where they're coming from," Cooper added. "Old ranger station about three miles in. Been deserted for years, but now it's crawling with activity. Looks like they've turned it into some kind of base camp."

Elijah straightened, his interest piqued. "We need to investigate that location. If they've established a central command post, it could provide crucial insights into their organizational structure."

"Too dangerous right now," Cooper advised. "They've got sentries posted in a perimeter around the station. Anyone approaches, they sound an alarm—not normal monkey screeching, but it sounds to me like specific patterns. Different calls for different threats."

This information confirmed what McKenna and Elijah had already observed about the macaques' developing communication system when they were out in the field, and during the clinic attack.

McKenna turned to address the tracker directly. "Mr. Cooper, in your estimation, how many macaques are we dealing with?"

He considered the question with professional seriousness. "Based on track patterns and territory markings, I'd say at least two hundred active individuals, possibly more. They're organized in what looks like specialized units—scouts, what you might call assault teams, and support groups that handle resource transportation."

"Two hundred," McKenna repeated, letting the number sink in. She turned to the mayor and Sheriff Harding. "We need to understand the scale of what we're facing. This isn't a small group of aggressive animals. This is an organized force with dangerous capabilities and the numbers to back them up."

Mayor Holden's composure slipped momentarily, her carefully maintained public persona cracking under the weight of this information. "Two hundred intelligent, tool-using primates targeting our town. How do we possibly manage that with our resources?"

"Remember," the sheriff said. "We've got help on the way."

"When, exactly?" McKenna asked.

Before anyone could answer, Deputy Alfaro burst through the gymnasium doors, his usual professional calm shattered. "Sheriff! We've got a situation at the Peterson property on Magnolia Street. Needs immediate response."

The urgency in his voice cut through all other activity. Harding moved quickly, McKenna and Elijah following close behind as they headed for the patrol cars outside. Vivian wanted to join them, but McKenna told her to stay put in case her expertise was needed at the base.

The seven-minute drive to Harold Peterson's modest bungalow passed in tense silence, broken only by radio updates that revealed little beyond "possible fatality" and "secure the scene." The words hung in the air like smoke, obscuring the full horror that awaited them.

Yellow police tape fluttered in the gentle morning breeze, a garish intrusion on the property when they arrived. Two deputies maintained a perimeter around what had once been Harold Peterson's pride—a garden that had won the county fair's "Best Maintained" ribbon three years running. The 78-year-old former postal worker had tended these beds with arthritic hands every morning for fifteen years since retirement, his knowledge of horticulture dispensed freely to anyone who'd listen. And many who'd pretended to.

Now the garden had a new centerpiece.

McKenna felt something beyond dread settling in her stomach as they approached—a leaden weight of premonition that made her steps drag involuntarily across the immaculate lawn. A small group of deputies stood in unnaturally rigid formation, their postures betraying the wrongness beyond. They parted as Harding approached, revealing the tableau they'd been shielding from view.

Harold Peterson lay arranged on the garden path, not sprawled as a fallen man should be, but positioned with a horrifying symmetry. Arms extended precisely at forty-five-degree angles. Legs together, feet pointed outward at identical angles. Face-up, eyes fixed on the morning sky, reflecting nothing but perfect blue emptiness. Most disturbing was the complete absence of the expected death pose—no rigidity, no natural contortion. He had been placed, like a doll arranged for display. His withered hands were crossed carefully over his chest as if he were already in his coffin.

The wound across his throat gaped like a second, obscene smile beneath his gentle face—a single, perfectly horizontal incision. No hesitation marks. No ragged edges. Just one decisive cut that had opened his carotid artery with the efficiency of an executioner who understood human anatomy. Blood had pooled and congealed in a perfect semicircle, stopping at an unnatural border as though contained by invisible barriers.

Beside his right elbow lay the apparent murder weapon: his own pruning shears, arranged parallel to his arm, blades opened to precisely the width of his neck. The dried blood on the cutting edge had been partially wiped away—not cleaned entirely, but deliberately left visible, like a taunt.

The contrast between the violence and the setting created a cognitive dissonance that made McKenna's brain stutter. Murder shouldn't happen in places that smelled of lavender and fresh mulch. Death didn't belong among the orderly rows of nodding daffodils and carefully staked tomato plants that surrounded the body like silent witnesses.

"Jesus Christ," Harding whispered, his voice carrying the hollow resonance of a man who'd seen war zones less upsetting than this garden. He crouched to examine the scene without affecting evidence, his movements uncharacteristically hesitant.

McKenna noticed how the birds had fallen silent—not gradually as humans approached, but with the unnatural completeness that suggested predators. The garden held a stillness beyond mere absence of movement; it felt suspended, as though time itself retreated from what had happened here.

Deputy Carlson, the first responder, stepped forward. His uniform remained pristine despite the heat, as if even sweat refused to manifest in this wrongness. "Neighbor called it in. Said she saw Mr. Peterson come out for his morning gardening around 6:30, same as always. When he didn't come in for his usual coffee break at 8:00, she checked on him and found... this."

He gestured toward the body with a hand that trembled almost imperceptibly. "No signs of struggle whatsoever. No defensive wounds. Soil analysis shows only a single set of footprints—his own—leading to this spot. It's like he just stood there and... allowed it."

McKenna studied the scene with her veterinarian's eye, cataloging details her brain didn't want to process. The lack of arterial spray pattern despite the severed carotid. The absence of defensive wounds on hands that should have instinctively risen to protect his throat. The way Harold's expression remained placid, almost serene—no surprise, no terror frozen on features that should have registered at least one of those emotions.

As McKenna looked closer, she noticed additional details. Small, shaped mounds of soil had been arranged at precise intervals around the body—not haphazard disturbance but deliberately formed cones exactly four inches high. Between them, barely visible unless you knew to look, lay small deposits of macaque excrement—not randomly placed but positioned to form a perfect circle encompassing the body.

Most chilling was what sat atop each soil mound: a single red rose petal, taken from Harold's prized Heritage bushes. The juxtaposition of violence and beauty, of bodily waste and careful arrangement, created a ritualistic presentation that transcended even the murder.

This was ceremonial.

"The cut is precise—one continuous movement with significant force behind it," she observed, her clinical vocabulary a thin shield against horror. "This required understanding of exactly where to cut and how deep."

"Could a macaque physically do this?" Harding asked, looking at Elijah. The question lingered between them, heavy with implications neither wanted to confront.

The primatologist nodded solemnly. "Adult males have the strength. The anatomy—" he swallowed hard, "—the anatomy of their forearms allows for the necessary force application and precision. The cut angle suggests a right-handed approach from behind, consistent with macaque attack positioning."

He pointed to something McKenna hadn't initially noticed: a small series of scratches on the garden shed door—the now-familiar pattern they had documented at multiple locations.

"They marked the site," Elijah continued. "The pattern has evolved. It's more complex, more... specific to this location."

Deputy Miller emerged from behind the shed, his face ashen. "Sheriff, we found something else. There's a... viewing platform in the oak tree overlooking this exact spot. Freshly constructed. Branches woven together to create a hidden observation post with direct sight-line to where the body is positioned."

The implication settled over them like a pall: the killers had not only executed Harold with terrifying precision but had arranged to watch the discovery of their handiwork.

McKenna felt seen, evaluated, measured by eyes that might still be watching from the surrounding trees and rooftops.

The reality of what they were facing crystallized in that moment—not just property damage or intimidation tactics, but methodical, calculated elimination of human targets selected through criteria they couldn't yet understand. Why Harold? What had made this gentle, elderly gardener their target?

"We need to evacuate the most vulnerable residents," McKenna said, her voice steady despite the nauseating terror climbing her throat. "Anyone living alone, especially near the preserve edge, needs to be moved to designated safe houses immediately."

She thought of the retirement home, of her own house, which was close to the de facto preserve. She turned her attention to the sheriff. "What about the construction site? Has the developer been warned?"

As she spoke, her gaze was drawn to movement at the periphery of her vision—a shadow shifting behind a neighboring fence, too deliberate to be wind-blown foliage, too small to be human. When she turned fully, nothing remained but the unsettling certainty of having been observed and assessed.

Harding nodded, already on his radio coordinating the response, his voice carrying the strained composure of a man forcing procedure to overcome primal fear. As deputies secured the scene and prepared for the medical examiner's arrival, McKenna became drawn to something odd about the garden itself.

The normally immaculate flower beds showed signs of disturbance—not random destruction or even simple harvesting, but what she guessed was careful extraction of specific plants. Entire species had been removed with care, leaving behind perfectly cylindrical holes where roots had been excised completely intact. The soil around these excavations wasn't scattered but neatly piled in small, geometric arrangements.

"Elijah," she called softly, indicating the disturbed soil. "They took something. Something specific."

He examined the areas she indicated, recognition dawning in his eyes like a man connecting points in a mystery plot. "These aren't just ornamental beds—these are medicinal plant beds. Harold was growing therapeutic herbs—echinacea, valerian, St. John's wort..."

He pointed to one particularly disturbed section where the soil had been not just excavated but altered—darker, almost black, with a network of fine white filaments visible in the exposed layers. "And this was likely a fungal cultivation area. I bet some gardeners grow medicinal mushrooms alongside their herbs. But these excavation patterns... they knew exactly what they were looking for."

"They're collecting components," McKenna realized, a new dread blooming as the implications unfurled. "Expanding their pharmacological resources. Harold wasn't just killed—he was harvested."

The dual purpose of the murder revealed itself with emetic clarity: demonstration of capability combined with resource acquisition. The retiree's death wasn't merely elimination of a human target but a calculated operation with multiple objectives—a level of conspiracy that overtook animal behavior and entered the realm of combat and plunder. She wondered if the breaking of ground in the new construction area had disturbed some of the macaques' own hidden gardens, forcing them to forage here.

McKenna felt the presence of invisible observers tracking their departure, cataloging their responses, measuring their fear. Harold Peterson wouldn't be the last. The carefully arranged petals, the precisely positioned body, the methodical extraction of specific plants—all of it spoke to a plan unfolding according to parameters they couldn't yet comprehend.

As they returned to the patrol car, McKenna's phone vibrated with an incoming call from Vivian.

"McKenna?" Vivian's voice carried unusual tension. "The Natural Balance people have gone to the preserve edge to 'establish peaceful contact' with the macaques. Justin convinced about fifteen people to join him at the eastern entrance."

"Tell Sheriff Harding's team at the command center," McKenna instructed. "We're still at Harold Peterson's place. He's been killed—throat cut with his own garden shears."

Vivian's sharp intake of breath carried clearly over the line. "My God. He was such a sweet old man. Why'd they kill him?"

"Not sure. Precision attack, no defense wounds. They marked the site with their symbols." McKenna climbed into the patrol car as Harding finished giving instructions to his deputies. "We're heading back now."

As they drove, McKenna stared dully at the homes they passed—places she had visited countless times for house calls, treating family pets and dispensing routine advice. Each house now represented potential vulnerability, each garden a possible ambush site. The small town she had chosen for its peaceful isolation had become the front line in an unprecedented conflict.

"What are you thinking?" Elijah asked, noticing her expression.

McKenna chose her words carefully, aware of Sheriff Harding beside them. "I'm thinking that we're not equipped for this—not tactically, not psychologically. We treat these macaques as aggressive animals because that's a framework we understand. But they're operating with a different kind of intelligence now. They understand our vulnerabilities in ways we don't understand theirs."

Harding's grip tightened on the steering wheel. "Are you saying we can't win this?"

"I'm saying we need to stop thinking about it as a threat that we can manage. We need to understand what they want, what they're trying to achieve beyond immediate objectives." She turned to face him directly. "And we need to act fast, because they're learning from every encounter while we're still struggling to accept what they've become."

As they approached the command center, a plume of dark smoke rose from the direction of the eastern preserve entrance where Justin and his misguided activists had gone seeking peaceful contact. Even from a distance, McKenna could see emergency vehicles racing toward the scene, lights flashing against the mid-morning sun.

The resistance had begun in earnest. But as McKenna watched the smoke rise, she wondered if resistance alone would be enough against an enemy that adapted with every passing hour—an enemy that had now demonstrated its willingness to kill.

# CHAPTER 8

Sheriff Lucas Harding pinned another incident marker to the large town map spread across the command table. Red for attacks on people, blue for infrastructure damage, yellow for thefts. The pattern was becoming troublingly clear. Four days into the crisis, the map looked like a battlefield assessment, which, he supposed grimly, was exactly what it had become.

The gymnasium hummed with activity around him—volunteers manning the sputtering landlines, deputies coordinating patrol schedules and fortifying roadblocks to keep out of town looky-loo's at bay, personnel from other sheriff departments doing what they could, and Mayor Holden attempting to maintain some semblance of civil authority while fielding increasingly urgent calls from state officials who seemed unable to grasp the nature of their situation. Social media posts couldn't be stopped, and the animal rights groups had put out their own press releases, but the area was still surprisingly well-contained.

Harding had abandoned his filthy regulation uniform shirt for a black t-shirt—Bowie "Serious Moonlight" Tour, 1983—that allowed greater mobility, though he kept his badge pinned prominently on his belt beside his sidearm.

"Cooper," he called to the hunter who had quickly proven invaluable in tracking macaque movements. "Reports of activity near the water treatment plant. Take Team Three and investigate, but observe only. No engagement unless directly threatened."

Cooper nodded, gathering his volunteers—all experienced outdoorsmen armed with non-lethal deterrents. Harding had established strict protocols after Peterson's death: no one operated alone, all teams maintained radio contact, and lethal force was authorized only in immediate defense of human life.

He checked his watch—10:17 AM. His body was holding up for now, fueled by strong black coffee and the focused clarity that emergency situations always triggered in him. Twenty-two years in law enforcement, including three tours as a military police officer before settling in Cypress Grove, had prepared him for crisis management. But nothing in his experience matched the surreal nature of their current threat.

His satellite phone rang—the only reliable communication link since most of the cell towers, phone lines, and internet connections around town had been mysteriously disabled. The caller ID showed the Florida Emergency Management Agency.

"Harding," he answered, stepping away from the command table for privacy.

"Sheriff, this is Regional Director Alvarez. I've reviewed your situation reports and resource requests. I need to be straight with you—we're stretched thin statewide. Wildfires in the Panhandle have three counties under evacuation orders. The governor's declared emergency status for both situations, but assets are limited."

Harding clenched his jaw, having anticipated this response after his third unanswered request for National Guard support. "Director, I understand resource constraints, but we have an unprecedented situation here. These are not normal animal attacks. We've had one fatality, multiple injuries, and targeting of critical infrastructure."

"I understand, Sheriff, but frankly, reports of 'militarized monkeys' are being met with skepticism at higher levels. We'll dispatch our own wildlife management specialists as soon as they're available, likely within 72 hours."

"We may not have 72 hours," Harding replied, keeping his tone measured despite his irritation. "These macaques are demonstrating tactical intelligence and coordinated strikes against vulnerable targets. We need immediate reinforcement."

"I'll escalate your request again," Alvarez promised, though her tone suggested limited confidence. "In the meantime, maintain defensive positions and document everything. Video evidence would help your case considerably."

After ending the call, Harding allowed himself five seconds of controlled anger—five seconds to acknowledge the absurdity of trying to convince bureaucrats that their small town faced a threat beyond conventional understanding. Then he compartmentalized the emotion, locking it away where it wouldn't interfere with his responsibilities.

Across the gymnasium, he spotted Dr. Dubrow and Dr. Jackson hunched over laptops at their designated research station. Despite the chaos of the past days, they had maintained scientific focus, methodically documenting the escalating macaque behavior patterns and analyzing attack methodologies. Harding had initially been skeptical of Jackson's academic approach, but the primatologist had proven himself admirably practical, his theoretical knowledge translating effectively to usable applications.

"Sheriff," McKenna called, waving him over with urgency. "We've identified a pattern in the infrastructure attacks."

Harding joined them, noting the fatigue evident in both scientists' faces. Neither had slept properly since the clinic attack, yet they maintained remarkable fortitude—a resilience he respected.

"Look at the chronology," Elijah explained, indicating a timeline superimposed over a utilities map of Cypress Grove. "They began with infrastructure—cell towers, internet nodes, radio antennas. Then electrical distribution points, starting with outlying areas and moving inward. Now they're focusing on water infrastructure—pumping stations and treatment facilities."

"Systematic degradation of essential services," Harding observed, immediately grasping the strategy. "Isolate, then debilitate, then control access to critical resources. Standard siege tactics."

McKenna nodded. "They're executing a campaign plan to make the town untenable for human habitation. Each stage creates new vulnerabilities that they can exploit in the next phase."

"Based on the pattern progression," Elijah added, "we predict they'll target food storage and distribution next—grocery stores, the school cafeteria, community pantries."

Harding immediately began adjusting defensive deployments in his mind, prioritizing the protection of these newly identified targets. "We need to harden these locations immediately." He turned to the cluster of his officers. "Deputy Miller, reassign Teams Four and Six to grocery store protection. Johnson, coordinate with public works to secure the remaining water infrastructure."

As his deputies mobilized, Harding turned back to the doctors. "What's their endgame here? Territory control? Forced human evacuation?"

"Unclear," Elijah admitted. "But their tactics suggest they're creating conditions where humans either abandon the area or become dependent on resources the macaques control. It's sophisticated intentional thinking—pressure points rather than direct confrontation where they'd be disadvantaged."

McKenna straightened, tucking a strand of stringy hair behind her ear. "There's something else to consider, Lucas. As sophisticated as their tactics appear, these macaques are operating within a limited conceptual framework."

Harding raised an eyebrow, waiting for her to continue.

"They've never been outside Cypress Grove. To them, this town likely represents the entirety of human civilization." Her eyes held a steady belief that Harding found unexpectedly reassuring. "They're smart enough to coordinate attacks on infrastructure, but not sophisticated enough to understand the broader context. They don't comprehend that even if they control this town completely, it changes nothing in the larger world."

Harding considered this, feeling the first glimmer of strategic advantage he'd had in days. "They don't know reinforcements will eventually come."

"Exactly. They can't conceptualize state borders, governmental hierarchies, or our military response capabilities. Their worldview ends at our town limits." McKenna tapped the map boundary. "They're fighting to control what they believe is everything, when it's really just a tiny dot on a much larger map."

A thin smile crossed Harding's face as he processed this insight. The macaques' intelligence had a ceiling—and that limitation might be their best weapon.

A commotion erupted at the gymnasium entrance as McKenna's daughter burst through the doors, moving with such purpose that the deputies stationed there barely had time to react.

Kira Dubrow had exchanged her usual fashionable attire for practical jeans and a sweatshirt, her short blonde hair pushed back with a headband. She clutched her phone like it contained vital intelligence.

"Mom!" she called, weaving through the command center with the single-minded determination unique to teenagers. "You need to see this!"

McKenna met her halfway, concern evident in her expression. "Kira, what are you doing here? You're supposed to be at Marjorie's house."

"This is important," Kira insisted, thrusting her phone forward. "It's all over TikTok and YouTube. Macaque videos from right here in Cypress Grove."

Harding joined them, his attention immediately focused. "Videos? Recent ones?"

Kira nodded emphatically. "Posted in the last few hours. From kids at school who've been watching the monkeys when their parents aren't around. They've been going out to the preserve edge and recording them."

"How are they even getting through?" Harding wondered aloud. Of course, he realized that some comm systems still remained intact, and signals were spotty, but still there in other areas.

She pulled up a video on her phone, and Harding leaned in to watch over McKenna's shoulder. The footage, though shaky, clearly showed about fifteen macaques in a clearing near the old ranger station. The footage documented something profoundly disconcerting—macaques arranged in formation, using sticks and stolen tools to practice coordinated movements. One larger macaque, recognizable as the scarred leader they had identified as Alpha, directed the others with specific gestures and vocalizations.

"Jesus," Harding muttered, watching as the macaques demonstrated what could only be described as combat drills—approach patterns, flanking maneuvers, and tool-based attacks on crude effigies of human beings.

"There are a lot of these videos," Kira explained, swiping to show another clip. "Different locations, different groups, but all showing the same kind of thing. And the comments are insane—people think it's some kind of movie promotion or a hoax. Some are even cheering the monkeys on, like it's funny."

Kira's face paled as she swiped to another video, her fingers trembling slightly against the screen. The image that loaded was markedly different from the previous ones. Harding leaned in closer, his initial disbelief quickly settling into a cold resolve.

The video was a shocking display that had somehow slipped through the platform's content filters. There, in ghastly detail, was Earl Simmons' body, strung up on a tree like a grim, real-life scarecrow. The once-tetchy fisherman was now a lifeless effigy—a gruesome warning from the macaques to the townsfolk of Cypress Grove.

Earl's limbs had been contorted and secured with crude bindings, his face frozen in a rictus of terror. The macaques had adorned him with symbols—sharp lines and circles etched into his skin with a level of precision that suggested shock-intent rather than indiscriminate violence.

The video had been filmed from a distance, the person behind the camera whispering in hushed tones to their viewers, but the image was clear enough. In the background, a chorus of macaque calls could be heard—cheering, almost, in their triumph.

McKenna's hand flew to her mouth, stifling a gasp. "Oh, God," she breathed out, her eyes wide with horror and disbelief.

Harding felt a surge of anger and sorrow, a mix of emotions that he had learned to compartmentalize over his years in law enforcement. "Kira," he said gently, his voice steady despite the turmoil inside him, "I need you to show me everything. And we need to get these videos transferred to my laptop—can you do that?"

As Kira nodded numbly, Harding turned to the Mayor, who was sitting by the phone bank. "Patricia, get on the horn with every media outlet within a hundred miles. Tell them we have videos now, and it's deadly serious. I want every influencer and news anchor to understand that this isn't a game or a hoax. We're in a fight for this town's survival."

He looked back at the screen, at Earl's body swaying gently in the wind, and made a silent vow. This would not be the future of Cypress Grove. He would do everything in his power to ensure it. "This is exactly what FEMA needs to see to understand what we're dealing with."

Elijah had joined them, his expression intensifying as he watched the footage being replayed on Kira's phone.

"Can we trace who posted these?" Harding asked Kira. "We need to find these kids before they get themselves killed for social media fame."

"Most of them are using anonymous accounts," Kira replied, "but I recognize some locations. That's behind the Alfaros' farm, and this one's definitely at the old quarry."

As they discussed the videos, a deputy approached with a concerned expression. "Sheriff, you should know—those Natural Balance activists are setting up some kind of demonstration at the town hall. They've got their own videos of the macaques they're showing on a projector. Calling them 'evidence of higher primate consciousness deserving protection.'"

Harding suppressed a surge of fury. Justin Reeves and his unhinged crusaders had continued their protests despite the escalating danger, seemingly oblivious to the reality of what they faced. Instead, they had doubled down, recruiting more supporters through propaganda highlighting the macaques' intelligence without acknowledging their aggression.

"Keep monitoring them," he instructed Johnson. "As long as they stay peaceful and don't interfere with emergency operations, they have the right to protest. But the moment they encourage dangerous behavior, shut it down."

Turning back to McKenna and Elijah, he gestured toward the command table. "Let's use these videos to update our assessment. If we can identify training locations, we might be able to cut them off at the pass."

For the next hour, they worked methodically through the footage Kira had discovered, mapping locations and analyzing behavior patterns. The videos confirmed what they had suspected but had been unable to document—the macaques were implementing a sophisticated campaign, with specialized units performing specific functions within a coordinated strategy. They had established what appeared to be training centers in remote areas, command posts for operational planning, and forward observation points throughout the town.

"Sheriff!" Deputy Miller called from the communications station, interrupting their analysis. "Just got word from the hospital. Two more injuries reported—workers at the north side pumping station. Apparent attack by approximately ten macaques using weapons."

Harding immediately dispatched a response team of what few personnel were not otherwise engaged, then turned to McKenna. "It goes without saying, we need to get these videos to state officials immediately."

"I'll compile the most compelling evidence and send it through your satellite connection," she agreed, already selecting key clips that demonstrated the macaques' capabilities.

Kira, who had been assisting them in cataloging the videos, suddenly frowned at her phone. "That's weird. The videos are disappearing."

"What do you mean, disappearing?" Harding asked.

"They're being taken down from the platforms. 'Content violated community guidelines' messages on some, others just gone." She refreshed several pages, growing more concerned. "They were all here before. Now almost half are gone. I ripped some and got them on the laptop, but the connection is real slow..."

Elijah looked up sharply from his tablet. "Is it possible the platforms are removing them because they look like fakes?"

"Maybe," Kira conceded, "but it's happening too fast across different platforms all at once. And only the ones showing military-type stuff are being targeted. The dead guy, I snagged that one first, so we have it. The ones of macaques just stealing stuff or breaking into buildings are still up."

A chill ran through Harding as he considered the implications. "Can macaques use computers?"

McKenna nodded. "We think so. I mean, it's possible. We don't really know just how deep their intellect goes just yet."

Harding considered this. "Can they access the internet?"

"With sufficient cognitive enhancement and observation of human behavior, potentially," Elijah admitted. "Especially if they captured devices during their raids. The interface would be challenging but not impossible with their level of dexterity and apparent intelligence."

"They're controlling the narrative," McKenna realized, the color draining from her face. "Removing evidence of their true capabilities while allowing footage that portrays them as merely disruptive rather than strategically threatening."

Harding's tactical mind immediately grasped the significance. "Information warfare. They're manipulating external perception to delay outside intervention." He turned to Deputy Alfaro. "Secure my laptop in the evidence lockup. Nothing gets uploaded without direct authorization."

As his team scrambled to implement these instructions, Harding felt the weight of command pressing down with renewed force. They weren't just fighting a physical threat but an adversary capable of understanding and manipulating human systems—including digital ones—to their advantage.

"Sheriff," McKenna said quietly, joining him at the command table. "If they understand information control at this level, we need to consider what other human systems they might be able to exploit. Banking, utilities control systems, emergency response networks."

Harding nodded grimly. "Already on it. I've had someone working with town IT services to lock down critical systems and implement physical authentication requirements." He tapped the map where their remaining assets were marked. "We're maintaining old-school redundancies—radio networks, physical message runners between secure locations."

Despite these precautions, Harding recognized the fundamental asymmetry of their situation. Human infrastructure and social systems had evolved with innumerable access points and vulnerabilities that only made sense in the context of human-to-human interaction. No one had designed these systems to withstand exploitation by non-human intelligence with human-level strategic thinking but animal instincts and physical capabilities.

The day progressed with methodical emergency management—securing critical locations, documenting incidents, coordinating volunteer efforts to maintain essential services. Harding found himself falling back on military protocols from his MP days, implementing defense-in-depth strategies and rotating security details to prevent fatigue-based vulnerabilities.

By evening, they had established a reasonably secure perimeter around central Cypress Grove, concentrating the population in defensible zones with backup power and water supplies. Households in outlying areas had been encouraged to relocate temporarily to designated safe houses—the high school, the community center, and the two churches with sufficient facilities for overnight accommodation.

As darkness approached, Harding gathered his command team for the nightly security briefing. "Based on what we know, we expect increased activity after nightfall. Teams One through Four will maintain perimeter security. Teams Five and Six rotate for rest cycles. All communication through radio channel three, authentication protocols in effect."

He studied the tired faces before him—deputies who had been working almost continuously around the clock, volunteers who had stepped forward despite personal risk, specialists like McKenna and Elijah who brought crucial expertise to their defense efforts. Cypress Grove had revealed its character through crisis, with far more courage than panic, more cooperation than conflict.

"Remember," he concluded, "no heroics. We maintain defensive positions, protect our people, and document everything." He swallowed, reversing his earlier directives. "Shoot to kill any monkeys you see. Help is coming, but until then, we're the front line."

As the meeting dispersed, Harding took a moment to check his satellite phone—no new messages from state authorities. The promised wildlife management specialists remained unavailable, diverted to more "credible" emergencies. He'd tried to upload the video showing Earl's battered body, but the file was corrupted. Useless. He pocketed his device with controlled frustration, knowing that external reinforcement would likely arrive only after they had sufficient evidence of the threat—evidence the macaques seemed determined to prevent from reaching the outside world.

McKenna approached, coffee in hand. "You should get some rest while it's quiet. You've been up for almost forty hours, haven't you?"

Harding accepted the coffee with a nod of thanks. "I'll catch some sleep when the night shift is fully positioned. What about you and Dr. Jackson?"

"Rotating rest periods," she replied. "One of us monitors patterns while the other sleeps. Vivian's coordinating medical preparations at the community center in case we have more injuries."

Their conversation was interrupted by the harsh squawk of the radio on Harding's belt. "Sheriff, this is Cooper at Position Bravo. Movement detected at the eastern perimeter, multiple suspects, er, monkeys, approaching the Henderson, Martinez, and Woodward residences simultaneously."

Harding was already moving toward the exit, McKenna following close behind. "All units, this is Sheriff Harding. Multiple contacts on the eastern perimeter. Teams Two and Three respond, maintain protocol distance, lethal deterrents authorized."

The night air carried the heavy humidity of the Florida spring evening as they emerged from the gymnasium. In the distance, emergency lights flashed as patrol vehicles converged on the eastern residential district. Harding's truck was parked in the fire lane, and his keys were already in hand as he calculated response times and tactical options.

"I'm coming with you," McKenna stated rather than asked, climbing into the passenger seat. "Those households all have pets. The residents might hesitate to evacuate without them."

Harding didn't argue, recognizing the practical advantage of her presence. As they sped toward the reported incursion, he maintained radio contact with the responding teams, building a clear picture from their updates.

"Multiple macaques, at least fifteen per location... Coordinated approach from different directions... Using tools to breach security measures... Residents reporting attempted entry through windows and attic access points..."

They arrived at the Henderson property just as Deputies Miller and Crosby were evacuating the family—parents, two children, and a terrified golden retriever being hurried into a patrol car. The house behind them showed evidence of invasion—broken windows on multiple sides, the door partially pried open, the power connection to the building severed.

"They hit all three houses at once," Deputy Miller reported as Harding approached. "Same entry methods, same timing. Martinez family reports they were targeting the home office where the father works remotely for the water management district."

"Woodwards?" Harding asked, scanning the street for signs of continued threat.

"Evacuated safely. Cooper's team is securing their location now. Reports indicate the macaques were attempting to access the garage where Mr. Woodward keeps his hunting bow."

McKenna had gone to assist with the Henderson dog, calming the animal enough for safe transport. "They're targeting specific houses with specific resources," she observed as she rejoined Harding. "Knowledge access, potential weapons, infrastructure control."

A sudden crash from the Martinez residence two doors down interrupted their discussion. Deputy Johnson's voice crackled over the radio: "Movement in the rear yard! At least ten subjects retreating with materials from the house. Permission to pursue?"

"Negative," Harding responded immediately. "Maintain perimeter security. Document what was taken when the area is secured."

The strategic withdrawal of the macaque forces—for that was how Harding had come to think of them—proceeded with the same coordination as their attack. Within minutes, the immediate threat had subsided, leaving behind damaged homes and shaken residents.

As they supervised the evacuation of affected families to the high school shelter, Harding noted the precision of the attacks. The macaques had breached exactly what they needed to access their objectives, disabled security measures with minimal wasted effort, and withdrawn at the optimal moment to avoid direct confrontation with responding forces.

"They're getting more sophisticated," he observed to McKenna as they watched the last patrol car depart with evacuated residents.

McKenna nodded grimly, surveying the damaged homes. "No doubt about it. They knew exactly what was in each house and why they wanted it."

The implications were there, unspoken but understood. Their adversary was not merely intelligent but also adapting with disturbing speed, implementing lessons learned from each encounter to enhance their next operation. The question was no longer whether they could contain the threat, but whether they could adapt quickly enough to match the macaques' evolutionary pace.

As they returned to the command center, the radio crackled with additional reports. The pattern was clear: the macaques were instigating a comprehensive campaign to control critical resources and information while systematically degrading human defensive capabilities.

He found himself thinking in military terms he hadn't used since his service days—asymmetric warfare, force multiplication, strategic initiative. The terminology felt surreal when applied to non-human combatants, yet it fit the reality they faced with bloodcurdling accuracy.

Back at the command center, as he updated the incident log with the night's events, Harding confronted the reality of their situation with the clarity that had defined his law enforcement career. They were facing an adversary with animal capabilities but human-level thinking—a combination with no precedent in the manuals or emergency protocols that normally guided his decisions.

Yet underlying the professional assessment, a more personal question nagged at him: How did you defend against an enemy that could think like you but wasn't held back by your limitations or values? The macaques operated with instinctual efficiency, unhampered by moral considerations or social constraints.

The night stretched ahead, promising further adaptation from their simian adversaries. Harding checked his weapon, adjusted his radio, and prepared for another sleepless vigil. Whatever came, Cypress Grove would face it under his watch. They might lack external support or precedent to guide them, but they had one thing the macaques, for all their enhanced cognition, might not fully comprehend—the human capacity to protect their own against impossible odds.

The battle for Cypress Grove had evolved from curious anomaly to existential struggle. And Sheriff Lucas Harding intended to ensure that humanity would not be found wanting.

# CHAPTER 9

The emergency lights in the high school gymnasium cast harsh shadows across exhausted faces. McKenna finished applying antiseptic to a young boy's arm where a macaque had scratched him during an attempted home invasion. The wound wasn't deep, but any injury raised concerns about infection and potential disease transmission, though the cognitive enhancement of the macaques seemed to have come with improved health as well.

"All done, Tyler," she told the seven-year-old, whose wide eyes reflected the traumatic experience of being awakened by small, precise hands attempting to open his bedroom window. "You were very brave."

The boy's mother, still in her nightclothes with a hastily grabbed jacket thrown over them, clutched her son's uninjured arm. "Will he be okay? Could he catch something from them?"

"The wound is superficial," McKenna assured her. "We'll keep it clean and watch for signs of infection. Vivian has you on the check-in schedule for tomorrow morning."

As the mother led her son toward the designated family sleeping area, McKenna surveyed the gymnasium-turned-shelter. In the time since Harold Peterson's death, Cypress Grove's population had increasingly consolidated into defendable locations. The high school now housed over two hundred residents—primarily families with children, elderly citizens, and those whose homes were nearest the preserve edge. Vivian and the town's M.D., Dr. Thatcher, had established an efficient medical station near the locker rooms.

McKenna rubbed her temples, the ache behind her eyes deepening after so many hours on her feet. The gymnasium smelled of disinfectant layered over sweat, microwaved meals, and the scent of too many people and their pets sharing too little space. Sleeping bags and foam mats created makeshift neighborhoods across the polished floor, with personal belongings forming tiny territorial boundaries.

In one corner, a King Charles Spaniel dozed beside a toddler who was scribbling with crayons on the back of a cafeteria menu. Three cats had been sequestered in the coach's office after complaints about allergies and nighttime wandering. There were even some caged pets—fancy rats, bunnies, and a chinchilla—in the mix.

"Dr. Dubrow?" A gray-haired woman approached, arms loaded with paperbacks. "Thought you might want first pick from what we salvaged from the library."

McKenna selected a worn medical thriller, almost laughing at the irony. "Thanks, Mrs. Halstead."

Nearby, teenagers huddled in circles, playing cards or board games with the forced enthusiasm of people trying to forget their phones were useless black rectangles. A father read aloud from a *Chronicles of Narnia* book, his animated voices drawing a growing audience of children. The normalcy they attempted to create felt both heartbreaking and necessary.

Across the gym, Elijah conferred with Sheriff Harding over maps spread over a folding table. With laundry not being a priority, Lucas was now wearing Wranglers and a Nick Cave & the Bad Seeds jersey. Despite minimal accommodations, Elijah maintained his meticulous appearance—a trait McKenna had once found amusingly vanity-driven during their research days but now recognized as his way of maintaining control amid chaos.

Mayor Holden's voice cut through the general white noise, high and strained as she spoke into the satellite phone—their last reliable connection to the outside world. "Yes, Commissioner, I understand your concerns, but we need immediate assistance. The situation has escalated beyond local management capabilities. We have multiple injuries, two fatalities, and infrastructure attacks."

McKenna approached the command table as the mayor concluded her call, frustration evident in her tight expression and the absence of her usual political smile. Her skirt suit looked incongruously formal amid the emergency shelter setting, though she had finally abandoned her tight bun, her graying hair falling loose around her shoulders.

"Any luck?" McKenna asked, already anticipating the answer from the mayor's expression.

"Commissioner Daniels is 'deeply concerned' but focused on the highway closures," Mayor Holden replied, setting down the satellite phone with controlled deliberateness. "Apparently, multiple access roads to Cypress Grove have been blocked by fallen trees." She glanced meaningfully at Elijah and Harding. "Trees that show evidence of deliberate cutting rather than natural fall."

"They're isolating us," Harding concluded, adjusting pins on the map indicating the blocked routes. "Cutting physical access in addition to communications disruption."

"What about helicopters?" McKenna asked.

"I've requested them. And emergency crews from Oakridge and Pine Valley to clear the roads," Mayor Holden continued, "but their resources are stretched thin with their own unusual infrastructure issues." Her voice dropped lower. "Power substation failures, water pumping station malfunctions..."

"The macaques are expanding their operational territory," Elijah observed, the academic detachment of his tone belied by the concern in his eyes. "Implementing a regional strategy rather than just targeting Cypress Grove."

McKenna felt a chill despite the gymnasium's warmth. "They're preventing reinforcement by creating distractions in nearby communities." She turned to Harding. "Have we confirmed these are related to our macaques rather than coincidental infrastructure problems?"

"Cooper sent reconnaissance teams to check the Oakridge road blockage," Harding replied, running a hand through his unkempt hair. "They reported the same marking patterns we've seen here scratched into the tree stumps. It's them, all right."

McKenna's eyes swept over the map, the realization dawning on her. "They do understand," she muttered, fingertip tracing the boundaries of the preserve and beyond. "They're aware of the world beyond Cypress Grove." Her voice carried a note of resignation. "The goal post keeps getting moved... They're not just keeping us in; they're keeping help out."

Elijah's gaze met hers, a silent acknowledgment of their ever-escalating dilemma. The macaques' actions were no longer just a threat to the town but a calculated move against any potential aid. He made notes on his tablet, adding these new data points to their growing documentation of macaque tactics. "They're demonstrating strategic depth—understanding that effective siege requires not just containment of the target but disruption of potential relief forces."

The gymnasium doors burst open, admitting Darren Cooper and two of his scouts. The hunter moved directly to the command table, his camouflage clothing mud-stained and torn in places, evidence of difficult terrain traversed with urgency. Despite his disheveled appearance, Cooper's eyes remained sharp, his movements precise—a professional accustomed to high-stakes tracking.

"Sheriff," he acknowledged Harding with a nod. "Completed the perimeter reconnaissance as requested. It's worse than we thought."

He unfolded a hand-drawn map on the table, adding it to the official town maps already displayed. "They've established sentry positions here, here, and here," he indicated, marking locations with a grease pencil. "Each position staffed by at least five macaques with clear lines of sight to approach routes. They're using a relay system for communications—specific calls that carry information rather than just alarm."

"What about the ranger station site?" Elijah asked.

"Heavily defended," Cooper confirmed. "At least fifty individuals visible." He hesitated, then added, "They've fortified the position—sharpened stakes around the perimeter, elevated observation platforms, what looks like deliberate fields of fire for projectile weapons."

Elijah shook his head, speechless.

"There's more," Cooper continued grimly. "On our way back, we observed teams of macaques checking and disabling vehicles throughout the outlying neighborhoods—slashing tires, removing spark plugs, draining fuel tanks. They're eliminating our transportation options."

Sheriff Harding's radio crackled with a deputy's urgent report, confirming Cooper's observation. Three patrol vehicles at the eastern checkpoint had been found with cut brake lines and fuel system damage—precision sabotage.

"What about the roadblocks?" Harding asked. "Can we clear them ourselves?"

Cooper shook his head. "Not without heavy equipment. They've dropped substantial trees across all major access roads. Would take chainsaws and winch trucks, at minimum. And they're watching the blockage points—any attempt to clear them would face immediate opposition."

Mayor Holden slumped slightly. "We're completely cut off. So what do we do?" Her composure cracked, and a single tear ran down her cheek. "Why can't we just shoot all the damn monkeys?"

Cooper's weathered face remained impassive. "That's an option, ma'am, but with their numbers and positioning in trees and hidden locations—going aggressive could result in significant human casualties before we even made a dent."

The Mayor straightened, political instincts reasserting themselves. "We need to address the townspeople, prevent panic, establish rationing protocols—"

Her administrative planning was interrupted by a commotion near the gymnasium entrance. Deputy Johnson escorted a frantic-looking young woman toward the command table—McKenna recognized her as Amelia Nguyen, one of the Natural Balance activists who had been a constant presence at Justin Reeves' demonstrations.

"Mayor Holden," Amelia called, her voice carrying across the gym and drawing curious stares from sheltering residents. "You have to help! Justin and the others—they've gone to negotiate with the macaques!"

McKenna exchanged alarmed glances with Elijah as Sheriff Harding immediately stepped forward. "What do you mean, 'negotiate'? When did they leave? How many people?"

Amelia's words tumbled out in panicked bursts. "Justin said we needed to establish a truce before the situation went any further. He said your approach was making things worse, that the macaques were just defending themselves against persecution." She chewed anxiously at one of her fingernails. "Seven of them left about an hour ago. Headed for the ranger station with white flags and offerings—fruit, toys, some blankets. Justin said if we showed we respected their intelligence, they'd respond peacefully."

"An hour ago?" Harding confirmed, already reaching for his radio. "Cooper, did your team observe any human tracks approaching the ranger station during your reconnaissance?"

The hunter's expression darkened. "No. We had clear sightlines to all approach routes for the past five hours. No human movement detected."

"They must have taken a different path," Amelia insisted, her voice rising. "Justin got ahold of the preserve maps."

McKenna felt her stomach tighten with dread. If Justin's group had attempted to approach the macaque headquarters undetected, they could have wandered into ambush areas or surveillance zones without any of the precautions experienced scouts like Cooper would employ.

"We need to establish their likely route and initiate a search," she said, turning to Cooper. "Based on the maps, what alternative approaches might they have tried?"

As Cooper outlined possible routes on the map, Kira approached McKenna, her expression troubled. The girl had been helping Vivian organize medical supplies, showing surprising maturity in the crisis despite her usual disinterest in her mother's work.

"Mom," she said quietly, holding out her phone. "I just lost all signal. Not just a weak connection—completely gone."

McKenna took the device, noting the "No Service" indicator where bars had previously shown intermittent connection. She glanced around the room and saw other residents checking their phones with similar confusion.

"It's not just yours," she confirmed, returning the phone. "It looks like they've taken down the remaining cell tower, or they're using signal jammers." She caught Harding's attention, gesturing to the issue.

The implications settled heavily over the command table. Cypress Grove was now completely isolated—physical access blocked, devices disabled, vehicles sabotaged.

"We need to establish fallback communication methods," Harding decided, immediately coming up with contingency protocols. "Runner network between secure locations, visual signals for emergency alerts. Miller, get the emergency generators prepped—I expect we'll lose main power soon if this shit show keeps on going like it has been."

As the command team reorganized, McKenna pulled Elijah aside, lowering her voice. "What's the endgame here? What do you think they really want?"

Elijah's expression darkened, his academic detachment giving way to emotion. "They want to turn the tables, McKenna. The APEX program created something that was never meant to exist. Evolution's being accelerated right before our eyes. They're not just trying to secure territory or resources. They're systematically dismantling our advantages, studying our weaknesses, and developing countermeasures to everything that makes humans dominant."

McKenna felt ice spread through her veins. "They want to replace us?"

"Not replace," Elijah whispered, "subjugate. Make humans the lesser species. They've learned how we treat animals. Now they have the intelligence to implement the same dynamic, but with us on the bottom."

Their discussion was interrupted as Vivian approached, clipboard in hand. "We need to discuss supply allocation. At the current rates, we have about three days of essential medications for our existing patients. If we get more injuries..." She left the implication hanging.

McKenna nodded, immediately shifting to practical concerns. "Let's establish priority protocols and inventory all sources—local pharmacies, clinic supplies, private residences. We should send teams to secure anything we can use before—"

The lights flickered once, twice, then died completely, plunging the shelter into momentary darkness before emergency generators activated, casting the space in dim, yellowish light. The abrupt transition from bright fluorescents to minimal emergency illumination triggered scattered cries of alarm from the sheltering residents. Somewhere in the dark, a toddler wailed.

Mayor Holden immediately moved to the center of the gymnasium. "Everyone remain calm! Our emergency systems are functioning as designed. Please stay in your designated areas."

As the mayor continued reassuring the public, McKenna, Vivian, and Elijah joined Sheriff Harding at the command table, where he was already issuing adjusted security directives through the radio network.

"Main power substation is down," he reported grimly. "Backup generators at critical facilities will provide temporary coverage, but fuel supplies are low. We need to enact strict electricity rationing immediately."

Elijah studied the infrastructure map, his analytical mind already identifying priorities. "We should focus power resources on the medical station, communications hub, and minimal perimeter security lighting. All other systems can be cycled or shut down."

As they reorganized their diminishing resources, McKenna found her gaze drawn to the windows, where twilight had begun to settle over Cypress Grove. The familiar Florida sunset, casting long shadows, seemed suddenly ominous—darkness had become the macaques' ally, the time when their superior night vision and clandestine tactics gave them the greatest advantage.

"Any word from search teams on Justin's group?" she asked Cooper, who had just returned from coordinating perimeter scouts.

The hunter shook his head. "Nothing. We've checked the most likely routes out of town. No signs of human passage, no response to signals." His expression conveyed what he didn't explicitly state—the probability of finding Justin's group alive decreased with each passing moment.

Night fell completely as they continued preparations for extended isolation. The gymnasium settled into an uneasy rhythm—families clustered on makeshift bedding, volunteers distributing rationed supplies, deputies maintaining security rotations at entry points. The shelter's atmosphere balanced precariously between organized response and incipient panic, held together by the structured leadership of Sheriff Harding and Mayor Holden's reassuring presence.

Vivian had finally succumbed to exhaustion, sleeping on a cot in the corner while still clutching her clipboard. Kira had surprised McKenna by volunteering to help monitor the younger children, organizing quiet games and stories to distract them from the horror unfolding around them.

Finding a quiet moment, McKenna stepped through the gymnasium's side entrance where a deputy maintained watch. The moment the heavy metal door closed behind her, the darkness pressed against her skin like something tangible, something hungry. The night air carried the heavy scent of the region's vegetation—cypress and palmetto, stagnant water and loamy soil—unnervingly normal despite the crisis unfolding around them.

Cypress Grove lay suffocated in shadows, the power outage revealing how much they'd taken electricity for granted. Only the high school and community center showed signs of life, their generator-powered lights creating sickly yellow islands in a sea of absolute blackness. The darkness between felt wrong—too dense, too complete, as if light itself was being consumed rather than merely absent.

McKenna scanned the tree line, squinting into inky blots that seemed to move independently of the slight breeze. Something rustled in the bushes thirty yards away—a deliberate sound that stopped too abruptly to be natural wildlife. She waited, breath held, but whatever made the noise had gone still, watching.

Elijah joined her, offering a cup of lukewarm tea from the shelter's dwindling supply. "Cooper's team just reported in," he said, voice low and tight. "The macaques have established even more observation posts overlooking all major roads. One of his scouts found crude diagrams scratched into trees—they look to be maps of our patrol routes with timing notations, he said."

McKenna accepted the drink with a grateful nod, noticing how Elijah's eyes darted constantly to the darkness beyond the weak security lights. His academic composure had worn thin, revealing the fear beneath.

"When we switched to randomized schedules, they positioned permanent lookouts instead of mobile units," he went on. "When we implemented countersurveillance, they developed a signaling system that doesn't require direct line of sight."

The tea was bitter and grainy on her tongue. "I'm scared."

Elijah put his hand on her shoulder, and they stood in silence, absorbing the implications. The distant hooting of an owl carried across the darkened town—three calls, then there was a cry that was abruptly cut off. Something had frightened it into silence. Or killed it.

"We should get back inside," McKenna said. The hairs on her neck prickled and rose, that ancient instinct humans retained despite civilization's veneer—the knowledge of being prey in darkness, of being watched by hungry, patient eyes. "Night belongs to them now."

As they turned toward the gymnasium door, something small and dark darted across the edge of the security lights—a shape too deliberate to be wind-blown debris, too controlled to be panicked wildlife. In the same moment, a series of distant popping sounds echoed across town—small explosions or gunfire, impossible to distinguish at this distance.

"Eastern sector," Elijah identified immediately, his research experience in conflict zones evident in his quick assessment. "Near the water tower."

The deputy at the door was already radioing the command center, reporting the disturbance and requesting instructions. McKenna cast one final glance at the void beyond the security lights. For a fraction of a second, she saw multiple small shapes moving in synchronized formation across a distant rooftop, silhouetted against the faint orange glow of fires igniting in the eastern sector.

Inside the gymnasium, Sheriff Harding stood at the command table, his face haggard in the harsh emergency lighting that cast everyone in pallor and sharp, unnatural shadows. He was mobilizing a response team while maintaining shelter security, his voice strained but steady.

"Reports of explosions at three infrastructure points," he informed them as they approached. "Water tower, backup generator at the substation, and the fuel depot at Alfaro's farm. The timing was precise—all three occurred within forty-five seconds of each other."

The macaques weren't just isolating them now; they were methodically removing options, creating conditions where human responses became increasingly predictable and manageable. Classic siege tactics.

Through the darkened windows, flickering orange light painted the night in hellish hues—fires resulting from the explosions, creating new demands on their already stretched emergency resources. The macaques had timed their attack perfectly, using darkness to their advantage while human defenders struggled with limited visibility and communication.

Inside the shelter, the residents huddled in family groups on makeshift bedding of gym mats and blankets. The distant explosions had shattered the fragile calm, replacing it with the contagious anxiety of trapped prey. Parents clutched children closer, their whispered reassurances belied by the fear in their eyes. Elderly citizens huddled together, some murmuring prayers while others shared grim assessments based on past experiences—hurricanes, floods, the Cuban Missile Crisis.

"Just like '62," Mrs. Abernathy muttered to her neighbor. "They're testing our defenses before the main attack." She absently rubbed the Ace bandage around her wrist, seemingly reliving the monkey bite she'd received.

"I heard they took the Henderson boy," someone whispered in another corner. "Snatched him right through his bedroom window. Not a sound."

"My cousin in Oakridge says they found symbols painted in blood on the church door," a man insisted.

"They can read our minds," a woman said with absolute conviction. "That's how they know where we'll be. They got into the water supply with some Asian virus."

The rumors swirled and multiplied, rationality crumbling under the weight of sustained terror. Someone had drawn protective symbols on the floor near the west entrance with chalk stolen from the adjacent classroom. A small group had formed something resembling an altar with items they claimed would ward off the macaques—salt, crushed herbs, a silver letter opener arranged in patterns that resembled nothing so much as the symbols the macaques themselves had been leaving throughout town.

Through it all, Mayor Holden offered reassurances, focused attention on immediate tasks rather than uncertain futures, and most importantly, gave people things to do. "We need volunteers for the children's area... Who can help with meal preparation... Is anyone here experienced with emergency generators..."

McKenna watched the mayor's effective crisis management with newfound respect. Patricia Holden might prioritize tourism and public image during normal operations, but she understood crowd psychology and the importance of perceived control during emergencies. She was giving people purpose, direction, and the illusion of agency in a situation where actual options were rapidly dissolving.

As McKenna moved toward the medical station, she passed a window facing the eastern perimeter. Something made her pause, some subliminal movement at the edge of perception. She leaned closer to the glass, squinting into the darkness beyond the security lights.

For a moment, she saw nothing but her own reflection—wan, exhausted, bleary-eyed. Then a shape materialized just beyond the light's reach. A face, but not a human face. The scarred visage of Alpha, his opalescent eye catching the meager light with its unnatural glow.

He wasn't hiding or skulking at the perimeter. He was standing fully upright, deliberately visible, watching her watch him.

As their eyes met across the barrier of glass and darkness, Alpha's lips pulled back in that unnerving approximation of a smile. He lifted one hand, small fingers grasping something metallic that caught the light. A scalpel—one taken from her own clinic during the raid. With deliberate, almost ceremonial slowness, he drew the blade across his own palm, dark blood welling in its wake.

Then he pressed his bleeding hand against the glass, leaving a perfect print—five fingers splayed wide, the blood trickling downward in rivulets that formed patterns that had McKenna wondering if they were too deliberate to be random. A message? No, a pledge.

When she blinked, Alpha was gone, leaving only the bloody hand-print as evidence he'd ever been there. No one else had seen him. No perimeter alarms had sounded. He had come specifically to her, slipping through the safeguards as easily as walking through air.

# CHAPTER 10

The realization settled into McKenna's aching bones with leaden finality. They weren't just under siege by intelligent animals. They were being hunted by something that understood them, studied them, and was learning to think like them with terrifying speed. Something that moved through darkness as confidently as they moved through light.

As if to confirm this thought, the lights in the gymnasium flickered once, twice—then plunged the shelter into absolute darkness before the backup generators kicked in. In those seconds of perfect blackness, someone swore they heard soft scratching sounds at every window simultaneously. Someone else insisted they felt small fingers brush against their arm despite being nowhere near an exit.

The residents of Cypress Grove huddled closer together, the thin veneer of civilization wearing thinner with each passing hour. Outside, darkness reigned complete, and within it moved creatures that had learned to use that darkness as a weapon—patient, calculating, and above all, watching.

As the night deepened, McKenna stayed at the command table with Elijah, Sheriff Harding, and the core emergency management team, assessing their deteriorating position with ruthless honesty.

"We have serious limits when it comes to essential supplies," Deputy Miller reported, his voice thin and tired. "Water will go first if the tower damage is as extensive as initial reports indicate."

"Medical supplies for emergency treatment are adequate," McKenna added, "but maintenance medications for chronic conditions will be gone soon. Insulin, heart medications, and seizure control drugs are priority concerns."

"Defensive capabilities are holding, but not for long," Cooper assessed. "Ammunition is limited, non-lethal deterrents even more so."

Sheriff Harding absorbed these reports with the steady focus that had made him the town's anchor. "Our priority remains survival... We maintain essential services, protect our people, and document everything for when reinforcements break through."

The unspoken question felt like an arrow poised to strike—what if reinforcements didn't arrive in time? What if the macaques' strategic isolation proved more effective than their response capabilities? The siege dynamics were textbook—contain, isolate, degrade, then exploit vulnerabilities.

Elijah spoke gently but firmly. "We need to consider that external assistance may be prevented from reaching us."

"Are you suggesting we can't hold out?" Mayor Holden asked sharply.

"I'm suggesting we need contingency planning beyond waiting for rescue," Elijah clarified. "Including potential proactive measures to break the containment or negotiate terms."

"Negotiate?" Harding repeated skeptically. "With animals?"

"With cognitively enhanced primates demonstrating strategic thinking and coordinated action," Elijah corrected. "Their behavior implies potential for recognizing mutual interest scenarios."

McKenna considered this possibility, finding both hope and horror in the concept. "But that assumes they share our value frameworks or can comprehend abstract concepts like truce or territorial compromise."

"Nature's Balance believed they could be reasoned with," Mayor Holden noted, concern for the missing activist group momentarily overriding her innate political calculation.

"The difference between recognizing intelligence and understanding its nature," Elijah observed, "is two different things. "Justin's assumption may have proved fatal."

The late-night strategy session continued, balancing immediate security concerns with longer-term survival planning. Throughout the gymnasium, exhausted residents had finally succumbed to sleep, creating an illusion of peace that belied their precarious situation. Only the periodic radio checks from perimeter guards disturbed the uneasy quiet.

Eventually, McKenna was alone at the command table, reviewing maps and incident reports while the others grabbed snatches of rest. A small sound drew her attention to the medical station, where Kira stood watching her, concern evident in her young face.

"You should be sleeping," McKenna said gently, making space as her daughter approached the command table.

"So should you," Kira countered, studying the maps with surprising focus. Her hazel eyes glinted gold in the dim light. After a moment, she asked quietly, "We're in serious trouble, aren't we? Not just emergency, but actual danger."

McKenna considered sugarcoating the situation, then realized her daughter had earned better. Kira had shown remarkable maturity throughout the crisis, stepping up when needed despite her usual disinterest in 'boring' adult concerns. She deserved honesty.

"Yes," McKenna admitted. "They've cut us off completely and they're slowly wearing us down. Every move they make is calculated—they're not just smart, honey, they're strategic. And they're learning from everything we do."

Kira absorbed this with a thoughtful nod. "Like that history program Dad made me watch about ancient warfare. Cut our supplies, stop us in our tracks, then wait for us to weaken before the final push."

"Exactly like that," McKenna confirmed, surprised and impressed by the connection.

"But they're still monkeys," Kira pressed, searching for reassurance. "They can't keep going like this forever, right? They'll get tired or distracted or go back to normal behavior eventually?"

McKenna wished she could offer the comfort her daughter sought, but truthfulness prevailed. "Well, the cognitive APEX enhancement seems to support a need to conquer what they see as the enemy."

Kira's shoulders slumped slightly. "So we're basically waiting to see if help arrives before they decide to finish what they've started."

The blunt assessment, coming from her sixteen-year-old daughter, struck McKenna with unexpected force. Stripped of scientific terminology and tactical analysis, Kira had articulated their fundamental situation with stark clarity.

"That's the basics," she acknowledged. "But we humans have overcome stunning setbacks throughout history because we have an advantage they don't—historical precedent to draw from."

Kira's composure cracked, her lower lip trembling. "Mom, I can't stop thinking about Mr. Simmons. What they did to him..." She wrapped her arms around herself, as if trying to hold the horror at bay. "The video—it wasn't just killing. It was like... torture."

McKenna pulled her close, feeling the slight tremors running through her frame. The memory of Earl's ruined corpse haunted them all, but for Kira to have seen it... McKenna wished she could erase that image from her child's mind.

"What about Mr. Peterson?" Kira's voice came muffled against McKenna's shoulder. "Was it the same?"

McKenna stroked her daughter's hair, weighing truth against protection. "There were... similarities."

Kira pulled back, her face pale in the dim light. "I noticed something else. They're going after specific people. The elderly, like Mr. Simmons and Mr. Peterson. Mrs. Abernathy. And Tyler Martinez—he's so little. If his mom hadn't been right there..." She swallowed hard. "That means something, doesn't it?"

"It's consistent with predator behavior, especially in species learning to hunt." McKenna kept her voice steady, clinical. "They target what they see as vulnerable prey first. It's a way to develop skills with minimal risk."

"But these aren't normal predators." Kira's fingers twisted in the hem of her shirt.

The observation chilled McKenna. Her daughter was right. "No, honey. They're not."

"I tried calling Dad." Kira's voice sounded faint, fragile. "Before everything went down. I kept trying, but he never picked up. And now..." Tears spilled down her cheeks. "What if something happens and I never got to tell him—" She broke off, unable to finish.

McKenna's heart clenched. The divorce had been hard on Kira, and her relationship with her father was still complicated. Now, faced with their mortality in such stark terms, those unresolved feelings took on new weight.

"Come here, baby." McKenna pulled Kira into a fierce embrace. Her daughter felt so small suddenly, like when she was little and believed her mother could fix anything. "We're going to make it through this. I don't know how yet, but we will. And you'll have plenty of time to talk to your dad about everything you need to say."

Kira's arms tightened around her. "Promise?"

"I promise we'll face whatever comes together." McKenna pressed a kiss to her daughter's temple. "That's what matters right now."

They held each other in the muted light of the command center, mother and daughter against the darkness. Around them, the sleeping residents stirred and murmured, while outside, the night pressed close against the windows. Somewhere in that darkness, intelligent eyes watched and waited, but in this moment, McKenna focused only on the warm weight of her baby in her arms, anchoring them both against the tide of terror.

* * *

Sheriff Lucas Harding watched the first pale light of dawn illuminate Cypress Grove through the gymnasium's eastern windows. After four hours of fitful sleep on a cot, he felt marginally functional, his years of law enforcement crisis response having conditioned his body to operate on little rest. He sipped hot coffee from a foam cup, surveying the shelter.

Approximately two hundred and thirty civilians had taken shelter throughout the school—the majority packed into the athletics area, with overflow families housed in the cafeteria, library, and larger classrooms. The medical station in the southeast corner had treated seventeen injuries over the past twenty-four hours, none immediately life-threatening but collectively taxing their dwindling supplies. The command center occupied the northern end, where planning continued. Deputies and volunteers maintained security at all entrances, operating on rotating four-hour shifts.

By objective measures, they were managing the crisis efficiently. By realistic assessment, they were living on borrowed time.

Harding ran a hand over his stubbled jaw, already plotting the day's security priorities in his mind. Water conservation had become critical after the tower attack. Generator fuel would last another forty-eight hours at current usage rates. Food supplies were adequate but would require strict rationing. Their defensive perimeter had contracted to essential facilities only, abandoning the wider town to macaque incursions.

Deputy Miller approached, his uniform since abandoned for cleaner clothes. "Morning, Sheriff. Cooper's team reports activity near the eastern checkpoints. Looks like the macaques are moving something."

Harding nodded, immediately alert. "Get Alpha Team ready. Standard protocols—observation only, no engagement unless directly threatened."

As Miller moved to implement these instructions, the mayor joined Harding at the command table.

"Sheriff, the residents won't stop asking for updates," she said quietly. "They need reassurance that we have a plan beyond just waiting for help."

"We maintain essential services, secure our perimeter, and document macaque activities," Harding replied, knowing the response was inadequate even as he gave it.

The mayor's expression showed her recognition of these talking points as administrative placeholders rather than substantive action. "Lucas," she said, dropping formal address in a rare moment of candor, "we both know we're facing the impossible. These people deserve honesty about our situation."

Before Harding could respond, his radio crackled with Cooper's urgent voice. "Sheriff, eastern perimeter team reporting unusual discovery. You need to see this. Intersection of Palmetto Drive and County Road 19."

"Copy that. En route." Harding turned to the mayor. "I'll update when I have more information."

He gathered four deputies and headed for the eastern exit, where their remaining functional patrol vehicle waited. The morning air carried the usual heavy humidity, but the background sounds of town activity were eerily absent—no cars, no opening businesses, no casual conversations between neighbors, no cute monkeys begging for a treat. Cypress Grove had fallen silent as a grave.

As they approached the checkpoint, Harding spotted Cooper's team positioned behind defensive barriers, weapons trained outward but not firing. The hunter himself stood slightly apart, binoculars raised toward the intersection approximately one hundred yards ahead.

"What are we looking at?" Harding asked as he joined Cooper behind the barriers.

Cooper wordlessly handed him the binoculars, his hand tremoring almost imperceptibly. Harding noted the man's pallor—Cooper, a seasoned hunter who'd tracked dangerous predators across five states, looked ill. Whatever lay ahead had shaken him to his core.

"Just... look," Cooper whispered, pointing toward the telephone poles lining County Road 19.

Harding raised the glasses to his eyes, adjusting the focus until the scene came into sharp clarity. What he saw sent an icepick stab through his combat-hardened system, triggering flashbacks to war zones where enemy combatants left warnings for advancing troops.

Clothing hung from the poles at precise, mathematically spaced intervals—shirts, pants, jackets—each piece carefully arranged in a posture that mimicked human form. The garments weren't merely displayed; they were positioned with excruciating deliberation. Shirts stretched wide as though still containing invisible bodies, sleeves extended in supplication or warning. Pants with knees slightly bent, suggesting figures frozen mid-step.

Most alarming was their condition. The clothing bore unmistakable signs of violence—not haphazard damage but methodical desecration. The group's once-pristine Natural Balance t-shirts were now stained with dark, rust-colored patterns that formed crude symbols across the fabric. Justin's distinctive embroidered jean jacket hung from the center pole, the decorative stitching partially picked and rewoven into something that resembled a knife. Some garments appeared deliberately shredded in places that corresponded to vital organs—throat, heart, abdomen—while remaining perfectly intact elsewhere.

Bile rose in Harding's throat as he registered a sickly-sweet odor carried on the morning breeze—not quite decay, but something equally disturbing that his brain refused to fully process.

"Seven poles, seven sets of clothing," Cooper observed, his voice barely audible. "Matches the number in Justin's group. They've been arranged according to height, age, and gender. Exactly like they stood in their group photo on the protest flyers."

"Any sign of the owners?" Harding asked through a suddenly dry mouth, though he already anticipated the answer. His mind flashed unwillingly to memories of remote Afghan villages where insurgents left similar displays.

Cooper shook his head grimly. "No bodies, no conventional blood pattern visible from this distance. Just the clothing, deliberately displayed and..." he hesitated, "...altered."

"Altered how?" Harding pressed, the professional part of his brain forcing himself to gather all relevant intelligence despite the dread pooling in his stomach.

"Zoom in. See how they've been... manipulated? Pockets turned inside out but then sewn closed. Buttons removed and replaced with what looks like seedpods or small bones. Zippers interlaced with what might be hair." Cooper swallowed. "I've seen predator behavior my whole life, Sheriff. This isn't predation."

A vertigo-like sensation washed over Lucas as he realized: they'd been expecting the patrol. The macaques had anticipated exactly where humans would establish their checkpoint.

"They're communicating," he concluded, lowering the binoculars with fingers that didn't quite feel like his own. "Demonstrating consequences for unauthorized entry into their territory, but also..."

"Sending a message," Cooper said, a muscle twitching under his left eye. "But why leave the clothing and not the bodies? Why arrange them like... like they're still being worn by invisible people?"

Harding considered this question, the growing horror competing with his professional assessment. "A few possibilities. Psychological impact without providing evidence of specific violence. Keeps us wondering. Off balance. Preservation of the bodies for some other purpose. Or..."

He left the final possibility unspoken, but Cooper nodded in understanding, his face ashen. Territorial apex predators sometimes cached kills for later consumption. While the macaques were primarily plant and seafood eaters in their natural state, their cognitive enhancement might have altered dietary behaviors along with other changes.

But even this explanation felt woefully sparse against the elaborate display before them—less like practical scavenging and more like a ceremony conducting meanings beyond human comprehension.

As they watched, the forest edge stirred. The sheriff raised the binoculars again, his breath catching as shapes emerged from the tree line with fluid synchronization. The macaques moved in formation, their procession following precise angles toward the displayed clothing. Alpha led them, his furrowed face impassive as he directed units toward each telephone pole with silent gestures.

The macaques approached each garment with reverent care, their movements slowing as they reached the poles. Small hands carefully untied knots that had been secured at precise tensions. Others made elaborate gestures toward the clothing—not random movements but patterned sequences repeated at each site.

Every single garment was folded along exact lines, the creases aligned with geometric perfection. Some macaques produced small objects—stones, seeds, metal fragments—which they placed inside specific folds before securing the bundles with intricately woven plant fibers.

"This isn't just cleanup," Cooper whispered, transfixed by the scene. "It's like they're harvesting something."

"Perfect shot, Sheriff," whispered Deputy Alford, shouldering his rifle. "We could take out Alpha and half his lieutenants before they scatter. Permission to fire?" The crosshairs in his scope centered on Alpha's chest as the macaque meticulously folded Justin's prized jacket.

Harding placed a firm hand on the barrel, pushing it down. "Stand down."

Cooper nodded in agreement. "That's exactly what they're expecting. Look at their positioning—they're deliberately exposed, almost inviting an attack." He gestured toward the tree line. "But I guarantee there are others we can't see, watching for exactly that response. We fire now, we trigger whatever trap they've prepared."

"And Justin's group could still be alive," Harding added, though the display before them suggested otherwise. He scanned the tree line, noting how the macaques maintained clear sight paths back to the forest. "Those clothes are bait. The macaques might lead us to survivors if we follow them back to their territory."

"Or lead us into an ambush," Cooper countered.

"Either way," Harding said, "we're outmaneuvered here. They're showing us they can take hostages, display warnings, and conduct operations in plain sight—all without giving us actionable intelligence. It's too risky to engage without knowing what we're walking into."

He struggled to maintain professional detachment as he watched the macaques complete their ritual. The garments—now transformed into identical compact parcels—were distributed among designated carriers who positioned them at specific angles against their bodies before retreating toward the forest in formations that mirrored their approach.

The entire operation had taken less than five minutes, executed with such fluid coordination that it appeared choreographed. Not a single vocalization had been exchanged throughout—as though the entire ritual had been rehearsed or telepathically directed.

Before disappearing into the tree line, Alpha turned toward the observation post. Even at this distance, Harding felt that gaze—calculating, measuring, and somehow knowing exactly where the concealed humans watched from.

As the monkey melted back into the forest, Harding lowered the binoculars as sweat began to bead his forehead. The telephone poles stood empty against the morning sky, stripped of their macabre decorations yet somehow more ominous in their bareness. The message had been delivered, the rite completed.

And in its wake, an unspoken certainty settled over both men. Whatever had happened to Justin's group was more than simple self-defense.

"No recovery attempt until we have better reconnaissance," Harding decided, professional assessment overriding humanitarian instinct. "Document everything from a distance, maintain perimeter security."

The morning sun cast a harsh light on County Road 19, turning the asphalt into a shimmering black river that flowed toward the horizon.

As they prepared to return to the shelter, Deputy Alford called from his observation position. "Movement at the tree line, south side of the intersection. Multiple subjects, coordinated approach."

Sheriff Lucas Harding stood frozen, the binoculars slipping from his fingers and landing with a soft thud against his chest. The scene unfolding before him was a montage of horror that no amount of military or law enforcement experience could have prepared him for.

A group of monkeys emerged from the dense foliage to the south, moving with the same unsettling precision that had characterized Alpha's earlier ritual. But this time, they carried a burden that struck straight to the heart of the town's fragile humanity—Earl's disembodied head rested on a makeshift stretcher of interwoven palm fronds, the skin displaying a waxy pallor that spoke of death and decay.

The troop approached the telephone pole that had so recently displayed Justin's jacket like a taunting trophy. With a concurrent movement that belied any semblance of animalistic instinct, they lowered the grisly offering onto the patch of earth still indented from Alpha's pawprints. The head came to rest with its lifeless eyes staring up at the sky, the open mouth caught in a silent scream that would haunt Harding's dreams for the rest of his life.

A shiver shimmied down the sheriff's backbone as he tried to make sense of the animals' actions. Was this some form of twisted retribution? A message directed at the activists who had dared to challenge them? Or was it a warning to the rest of Cypress Grove—a demonstration of what was to come if they continued to defy the macaques' dominion?

The creatures retreated with the same silent efficiency as before, their forms disappearing into the shadows of the forest as if they had never been there at all. The stillness that followed was oppressive, the only sound the pounding of Harding's heart in his ears.

With a reluctant nod, Harding signaled to his team. They formed a protective circle around him, their rifles trained on the tree line as he stepped out from behind the makeshift barricade. The asphalt radiated warmth through his boots, and each step felt heavy, as though his feet were encased in lead.

As he approached the telephone pole, the smell of decomposition reached his nostrils—a cloyingly sweet, fetid odor that was unmistakable even over the lingering scent of morning dew. Earl's head lay in a bed of crushed grass, the once-shrewd eyes now clouded and vacant.

The sheriff's hands trembled as he reached out to retrieve the fallen man's head. He had seen death before, had stood amidst the wreckage of bodies shattered by war and violence, but this was different. This was personal—Earl had been a part of Cypress Grove, a fixture at the local diner where he always ordered the blue plate special with extra pickles.

With a deep breath to steady himself, Harding wrapped the palm frond around the head, shielding his own eyes from the sight of

Earl's final, frozen expression of unspeakable terror. It was a makeshift shroud, a small act of dignity in the face of inhuman brutality.

As he lifted the head, something glinted in the sunlight—a small object placed carefully beside Earl's severed neck. Harding leaned closer, his curiosity momentarily overriding his revulsion. It was a coin, an old silver collector's item that looked strangely out of place amidst the carnage.

The coin bore the mark of Cypress Grove's founding year, a relic that had once symbolized hope and prosperity for the small community. Now, it represented something else entirely—a harsh reality check that the monkeys were not just animals, but sentient beings capable of understanding, and perverting, human symbols and values.

# CHAPTER 11

The journey back to the gymnasium was a silent one, each member of the team lost in their own thoughts. The shelter awaited them, a sanctuary that felt increasingly like a prison. But for now, it was all they had—a thin shield against the encroaching tide of chaos and violence that threatened to engulf their town.

As they drove through the deserted streets, the sheriff couldn't shake the knowledge that they were running out of time. The macaques were sending a message, one that was clear and chilling. And if they didn't find a way to fight back soon, there might not be anyone left to mourn the fallen.

As they approached the school, Harding spotted McKenna Dubrow near the entrance, her expression shifting from general concern to focused attention.

"Sheriff," she called as he exited the vehicle. "Any sign of Justin's group?"

Harding met her eyes directly, professional respect demanding honesty despite the grim news. "We found their clothing displayed on telephone poles at the eastern perimeter. The macaques conducted a recovery operation while we observed, removing all evidence." He swallowed, his Adam's apple bobbing. "But that's not the worst of it."

McKenna's face paled as Harding relayed the morning's discovery.

"Earl's..." she trailed off, unable to complete the sentence.

"We left it at the morgue," he said, his voice steady despite the turmoil within. "But with the power situation..."

McKenna understood the implications. The refrigeration system was a luxury that could fail at any moment, and with it, their ability to preserve what little dignity remained for the dead. "The video... Do you think... there's more than what we saw the other day?"

"It's possible," Harding admitted. The possibility of a sequel hanging as-yet unseen in cyberspace was a sobering thought.

They agreed, for the moment, to keep the discovery of Earl's severed head from the general population. Panic was a virus they could ill afford to spread within the confines of their fragile sanctuary.

Together they entered the gymnasium, but Harding couldn't shake the image of Earl's gooey, sunken orbs.

Mayor Holden and Dr. Jackson were already coordinating morning activities—food distribution, medical checks, security rotations. The command team gathered at the table, where Harding provided an abbreviated briefing of their discovery and observations.

As he was speaking, a commotion erupted near the family sleeping area. McKenna's head snapped up at the sound of a woman's raised voice—Marjorie, who had been keeping watch over Kira.

"She was here when I fell asleep," the receptionist was explaining to Deputy Johnson, her silver bob disheveled from sleep and worry. "I woke up around 5 AM and thought she might be in the bathroom, but she never came back. I've checked everywhere."

McKenna moved toward them with gathering speed, Harding following close behind. "Marjorie, what's happening? Where's Kira?"

The older woman's distress was evident as she turned to McKenna. "I can't find her anywhere. She was sleeping right here beside me but then she was gone. I thought maybe she went to help someone else or find you, but no one's seen her."

Harding watched the color drain from McKenna's face, the steady-handed medical professional instantly replaced by a terrified mother. He immediately shifted into investigative mode, addressing Deputy Johnson. "Full shelter search, immediate priority. Check all rooms, closets, utility areas. Radio confirmation of all sections."

As the deputies and two civilians mobilized for the search, the sheriff turned to the school's head custodian, who had been assisting with facility management throughout the crisis. "We need access to any security camera systems still operational on backup power."

The custodian nodded. "Main office has the security hub. Cameras cover entrances and hallways. I think they're still running on emergency power, but I can't be sure."

"I'm coming with you," McKenna stated, her tone allowing no possibility of refusal.

The security office contained six monitors displaying grainy black-and-white footage from cameras positioned throughout the school. With power conservation measures in effect, only essential security cameras remained operational, creating significant blind spots in their coverage. The system stored approximately ten hours of footage on local hard drives, unaffected by the communications blackout affecting external connections.

"Start with exit points between midnight and 6 AM," Harding instructed the custodian, who began navigating the system in fits and starts.

The footage revealed standard shelter activity until 4:37 AM, when the gymnasium's side exit showed movement. A figure that Harding immediately recognized as Kira Dubrow appeared, moving with apparent purpose rather than under duress. She was followed by a young woman Harding identified as Emily Carson, one of the Natural Balance members who had been less vocal than Justin but equally committed to their cause.

"She left voluntarily," he observed, noting the absence of visible coercion. "With Ms. Carson."

While several of Natural Balance activists had gone to negotiate with the macaques at their headquarters, some had stayed behind. "Emily was helping at the children's area yesterday evening," McKenna said. "I wondered why she hadn't joined Justin and the others, but... She must have convinced Kira to go with her."

They followed the security footage through available cameras, tracking the two figures as they moved through the school's western corridor toward a rarely-used service exit. The final camera showed them slipping through the door at 4:42 AM, Emily checking for observers before closing the exit behind them.

"No security personnel stationed at that exit," Harding noted, cataloging the defensive failure. "It was supposed to be locked and alarmed, but the power outage must disabled the system there." He took a deep breath. "We need a focused search team. Small, experienced, armed but disciplined. Target area would be the forest edge, moving toward the most likely routes to the ranger station."

"I'm going," McKenna stated with absolute certainty.

"That's not a good idea, McKenna," he countered, though he had expected her response. "We need your medical expertise here, and your emotions could compromise things."

Her eyes hardened with determination that brushed aside diplomatic considerations. "She's my daughter, Lucas. Nothing you say will keep me here while she's out there."

Before he could respond, Elijah Jackson appeared in the doorway, his eyebrows raised. "What's happened?"

"Kira's missing," McKenna choked. "Security footage shows her leaving with one of those animal rights crazies—Emily—around 4:30 this morning. Heading toward the preserve, or maybe the ranger station."

Elijah absorbed this, then said, "Emily was asking questions last night about Justin's route. She mentioned having spent summers in Cypress Grove and knowing trails off the fire roads."

This new information shifted Harding's expression. "Do you know which routes she might have been referring to?"

"No, but I can try to help narrow the search parameters based on the territory marking we documented when I first got here," Elijah offered.

Harding weighed the variables against his dwindling resources. With most personnel and volunteers needed for shelter security and perimeter defense, a search operation would cause significant strain. But there really was no choice.

"Two search teams," he decided. "Cooper leads Alpha team taking the most likely route based on standard approach patterns. I'll lead Bravo team focusing on alternative paths Emily might have known about." He turned to McKenna and Elijah. "You two remain here to coordinate command operations during our absence."

"Not happening," McKenna replied flatly. "I'm going with Cooper's team."

"And I'll go with you," Elijah added with surprising firmness. "My knowledge of their territorial patterns will be more valuable in the field than here."

Harding recognized the futility of arguing. "Under protest," he conceded. "But you follow commands without question once we're in the field. Cooper's team leaves in ten minutes from the east entrance. Mayor Holden assumes command authority during our absence."

As McKenna and Elijah went to gather their things, Harding finished organizing the search parameters, designating team compositions and equipment allocations. Every asset deployed to the search meant defenses were removed from the shelter's protection—a calculated risk he hoped wouldn't prove catastrophic.

* * *

Thirty minutes later, Harding led his five-person team through the school grounds, moving with wary discipline toward the forest edge where they would begin searching alternative routes to the ranger station. Cooper's team, including McKenna and Elijah, had already departed, taking the more obvious approach path to cover maximum territory efficiently.

The morning had fully bloomed, bringing Florida's characteristic sticky heat that would make tracking more difficult as the day progressed. Harding maintained alert observation as they moved, noting signs of macaque activity throughout the seemingly abandoned town.

An hour into the search, Harding's radio crackled with Cooper's voice, distorted by interference but understandable. "Sheriff, we've found something. Approximately one mile northeast of checkpoint three, near the old fire road."

"Details," Harding requested, already signaling his team to adjust their pattern toward Cooper's position.

"Tracks showing two people moving east, followed by approximately six smaller sets indicating macaques in pursuit. Signs of struggle about half a mile in—a travel cup, disturbed vegetation, drag marks continuing deeper into the preserve."

Harding felt a cold certainty settling in his gut. "Any blood evidence or clothing?"

"Negative on blood. Tracking indicates subjects were taken rather than killed on site."

A small mercy, perhaps, though the outcome was still uncertain. "Maintain position, continue documenting. We're converging on your location."

As Harding's team altered course toward Cooper's coordinates, his radio erupted with urgent transmission from the shelter. Deputy Miller's voice carried unmistakable alarm despite his attempt at professional composure.

"Sheriff, we have multiple contacts approaching the shelter perimeter. Coordinated movement from three directions. At least thirty subjects visible, possibly more in covered positions. They appear to be carrying weapons and what look like projectile launchers. Permission to initiate defensive measures."

The timing couldn't have been coincidental. The macaques had waited until search teams deployed from the shelter, reducing defensive capability before launching their assault.

"Implement Defensive Protocol Charlie," Harding ordered, already calculating return time versus immediate threat assessment. "Secure all entrances, move civilians to interior rooms away from windows. Authorized use of deterrent measures only—no lethal force unless immediate life threat."

He switched channels, contacting Cooper's team. "Be advised, the shelter is under attack. This may be a coordinated operation to divide our forces. Maintain alert status and continue search effort, but prepare for potential engagement."

McKenna's voice came through, tense but controlled. "We've found more signs. Drag marks leading toward the ravine system east of the old quarry. Elijah says that area shows evidence of macaque activity in our previous reconnaissance."

Harding faced the commander's eternal dilemma—divided critical assets requiring simultaneous attention with inadequate resources for both. The shelter held over two hundred civilians dependent on his protection, while his most valued medical and scientific resources went into increasingly hostile territory.

"Cooper, maintain search operation with McKenna and Dr. Jackson. Exercise extreme caution—observation priority over engagement." He switched back to the shelter channel. "Miller, we're returning to defensive positions. ETA twelve minutes. Maintain perimeter integrity and civilian protection protocols."

As Harding pushed his team back toward the high school, adrenaline sharpened his focus. Between the houses, he caught flashes of what awaited them—dark shapes swarming the school perimeter like ants on a carcass. Some scurried along rooftops, others had claimed the tower and nearby buildings as sniper nests, raining down projectiles on the barricaded defenders below.

"Jesus," muttered Deputy Rodriguez, breathing hard beside him. "They're everywhere."

Harding's blood chilled as he recognized the pattern. Suppression teams pinning down the defenders while breach units probed for weak points. Wily tactics executed with inhuman precision and speed.

The radio crackled: "Sheriff, we're taking heavy fire at the main entrance. They're trying to punch through the cafeteria loading dock."

Two hundred innocent people trapped inside. And the macaques were closing in like a noose.

"All teams, be advised," he transmitted as they closed distance to the perimeter. "Macaques are implementing coordinated assaults. They're using elevated positions on adjacent buildings for ranged attacks while ground forces target entry points. Approach with caution and maintain cover."

They reached the athletic field bordering the school's western side, using the equipment storage building for cover as they observed the ongoing attack. From this vantage point, Harding could see at least twenty macaques engaged in the assault, operating in specialized units—some launching projectiles using improvised slings and catapults, others attempting to breach doors and windows using prying tools, still others maintaining perimeter security and communication relays between groups.

"They're focusing on the gymnasium's northern entrance and the cafeteria loading dock," Deputy Rodriguez reported as they joined forces at the perimeter. "We've maintained containment so far, but they're testing defenses, finding weaknesses, then concentrating force at the vulnerable points."

Harding integrated this information with his own observations, formulating response strategy as he moved toward the command position behind reinforced barricades. "Status of civilians?"

"All residents moved to interior classrooms and locker rooms. Mayor Holden is coordinating shelter operations. Medical station reports two injuries from rocks that got through gymnasium windows before evacuation."

Inside the defensive perimeter, Harding found controlled turmoil as deputies and volunteers maintained rotating defense positions while townspeople huddled in designated safe areas. Mayor Holden was in the central hallway, coordinating communication between sectors with admirable efficiency.

"Sheriff," she acknowledged his arrival with evident relief. "They began attacking just a few minutes after the search teams left."

"Any contact attempts?" he asked, though he anticipated the answer.

"No, nothing. They're just... attacking." She hesitated before adding, "But here's the thing that's really getting to me—they're not trying to kill us. I've seen them have clear shots at our people, and they deliberately miss. Hit the wall right next to someone's head instead."

"They're testing our capabilities," he said. "Or maybe just trying to wear us out."

As the commotion went on outside, Harding's radio carried Cooper's voice, transmission quality degraded by distance and interference. "Sheriff, we've tracked the drag marks to a ravine approximately two miles northeast of the old quarry. Found clear evidence of Kira and Emily being taken by a macaque unit toward what appears to be an underground entrance of some kind. Dr. Jackson thinks it may connect to the ranger station through natural cave systems."

"What are the options?" Harding asked.

"Limited," Cooper replied frankly. "The area is heavily monitored by sentries, with what appears to be a defensive perimeter. Dr. Dubrow wants to keep going."

Harding had expected nothing less. "Maintain observation position only. Do not attempt entry without additional support. Prepare extraction route options."

As he coordinated defensive measures at the shelter while monitoring the increasingly precarious search operation, Harding confronted the reality of their deteriorating strategic position. The siege continued to tighten its grip on Cypress Grove, with human defenders increasingly constrained by dwindling resources and multiplying threats. Somewhere in the forest beyond their defensive perimeter, McKenna pursued her missing daughter into territory controlled by an adversary that had systematically outmaneuvered every human response thus far.

* * *

Dr. Elijah Jackson moved with efficiency through the dense undergrowth, each step placed with deliberate care to minimize sound and disturbance. Years of field research in various environments had honed his ability to navigate challenging terrain while maintaining constant environmental awareness. Behind him, McKenna followed with surprising competence for someone whose primary work was clinical rather than field-based.

They had separated from Cooper's main search team twenty minutes earlier, following Elijah's assessment that the tracker's direct pursuit approach would be anticipated and monitored by macaque sentries. Instead, they were implementing a flanking route Elijah had identified based on behavioral patterns documented during their previous observations—a gap in the territorial surveillance system where the macaques' methodical coverage showed subtle inconsistency.

"The drag marks continue in this direction," McKenna whispered, indicating disturbed vegetation where the ground showed signs of something being pulled through the underbrush. "But they're not as deep."

Elijah studied the trail. "They're transitioning to carried transport rather than dragging. Like they constructed some kind of a stretcher."

McKenna's eyes burned with a fierce combination of scientific precision and maternal desperation—a mix that kept her functioning through hell. When Elijah had first arrived in Cypress Grove, it had been just another fascinating research opportunity. Now, watching her search for Kira with relentless determination, he found himself caring about a lot more than just the data.

Everything he thought he knew about evolution had been shattered in the past few days. These weren't just enhanced animals—they were something entirely new. The way they planned, adapted, learned from every human mistake... it defied everything in the textbooks.

The pieces were falling into place with horrifying clarity. The old APEX files, the cognitive enhancement compounds, the way each generation seemed smarter than the last. These macaques were the result of a military experiment gone wrong—or maybe gone exactly as planned. Enhanced intelligence passed down not just through bloodlines, growing stronger with each birth.

And now they had Kira.

"Elijah," McKenna whispered, interrupting his thoughts. "Look at this."

She pointed to a series of marks scratched into a cypress tree—the now-familiar symbolic patterns they had seen at multiple locations throughout Cypress Grove.

"Their communication system continues evolving," he noted, photographing the markings with his phone's camera despite the device's inability to transmit data through the blackout. "These incorporate positional references and numeric values—they're creating navigational guidance for their operational units."

"Can you interpret any of this?" McKenna asked, her voice tight with fear.

Elijah's hands trembled slightly as he traced the patterns. "This... this shows direction and distance. I can't tell how far. And these marks—they're counting something. Or someone." He pointed to a symbol that made his blood curdle. "That's Alpha's mark. He's been here."

Each step deeper into the foliage felt like descending into a nightmare. Everything Elijah thought he knew about intelligence, about evolution, about what separated humans from animals—it was all collapsing around him. The scientific implications should have thrilled him. Instead, they rocked him to his core. If intelligence could leap this far this fast, what did that mean for humanity's place in the world?

A stream appeared ahead like a lifeline. Elijah grabbed McKenna's arm, his heart hammering. "Perimeter boundary," he whispered, pointing to nearly invisible signs that screamed *organized intelligence.* "They're watching. Everywhere."

"How do we get through?" she gasped.

"The water." His field training kicked in despite his fear. "It's our only chance."

The stream felt like ice against their legs, but it was nothing compared to the chill that scurried down Elijah's spine when he spotted the observation platform. Perfectly camouflaged, mathematically precise, incorporating engineering principles that should have been beyond any animal's comprehension.

When the ranger station finally came into view, Elijah felt reality tilt on its axis. The structure before them wasn't an animal habitat—it was something else entirely.

"My God," McKenna breathed. "What have we walked into?"

# CHAPTER 12

E lijah studied the operation, his brain desperately trying to categorize what his eyes refused to accept. The macaques had established specialized work zones where small groups engaged in what could only be described as assembly line production—tool modification, material processing, weapons manufacturing. The stolen crossbow one of the residents had reported missing was there, as well as handsaws, hedge clippers, and two machetes. The efficiency of their movements suggested not just training but a deep understanding of process optimization principles.

Most unsettling were the storage systems visible near the main structure—not chaotic hoarding but meticulously categorized collections. Human items had been arranged not by obvious characteristics like size or color, but by apparent function and complexity. Tools with similar purposes grouped together, electronic components sorted by type, and personal items—watches, jewelry, identification cards—organized in patterns that suggested some unfathomable classification system.

"We need to get closer," McKenna insisted, already moving toward a section of bank where dense undergrowth provided the best cover. "Kira could be there."

The drainage ditch they used for their approach reeked of stagnant water and decomposing vegetation. As they crawled through the muck, the smell grew worse—not just organic decay but something chemical and wrong, like cleaning products mixed with rancid blood. The deeper they went, the more the smells changed, cycling through combinations that had no right existing together—antiseptic and rot, ozone and feces, formaldehyde and fruit.

Their cautious approach brought them within thirty meters of the station's rear wall. From this vantage point, new horrors revealed themselves in grotesque detail. What had once been a mundane government building now bristled with adaptive modifications that defied easy categorization—neither fully animal nor human in design, but something that existed in the uncanny valley between.

The walls had been reinforced with salvaged metal and car parts, but the arrangement followed no conventional engineering principles. Instead, the materials created patterns that simultaneously served structural functions and formed what looked like circuit diagrams or equations. Strings of collected items—bottle caps, keychains, small electronic components—hung at precisely measured intervals, clicking together in the breeze to create complex rhythmic patterns.

Then there were human belongings transformed into something new and bizarre—eyeglasses bent and rewoven into complex three-dimensional shapes, children's toys disassembled and reconstructed into mechanisms with no discernible purpose, clothing braided into rope-like structures that formed complex knots resembling neural networks.

"Look at the rear section," McKenna whispered, indicating a partially enclosed area attached to the main structure. "Those are cages."

Elijah focused on the indicated area, his stomach doing a flip as academic intrigue battled with existential fear. The macaques had created structures using materials that should not have held together—chain-link fencing woven with garden hose, wooden supports reinforced with automotive belts, locks modified from bike chains. Each enclosure held a single human occupant.

"The Natural Balance group," he confirmed, counting seven individuals. "Including Justin."

The captives were physically intact, though hollow-eyed with terror. Each had been provided with water in containers made from cut and sealed plastic bottles, but no food was visible. Their clothing had been removed and replaced with rudimentary coverings fashioned from bark fiber and plastic shopping bags, woven together in patterns that mimicked the macaques' own natural coloration.

Most unusual was what surrounded the captives—arrangements of small objects placed just outside each cage. Personal items arranged in patterns that seemed to correspond to details about each individual—medical prescriptions, photographs, driver's licenses. Identity markers. Classification systems. Study materials.

"I don't see Kira or Emily," McKenna noted, her voice tight with renewed anxiety.

"They may be held separately," Elijah suggested, continuing his methodical observation while fighting rising nausea. He fanned away the ever-present mosquitoes with his hands. "The macaques seem to be categorizing their captives according to some system we don't yet understand."

When they finally reached the cages undetected—a minor miracle given the sophisticated security patterns—the prisoners' reactions

were immediate and visceral. Justin Reeves made an abortive movement that McKenna stilled with a finger to her lips, his eyes wide with
a recognition that went beyond simple relief.

"Where's Kira?" she whispered urgently to the nearest captive, a
young man whose face had taken on the waxy pallor of profound
trauma.

"They took her and Emily underground," he whispered, voice
cracking with dehydration and dread. "There's... there's a whole system under the station. Old tunnels."

Elijah worked on opening an enclosure, noting with disturbed
fascination how the macaques had modified standard padlocks using
principles that showed an understanding of mechanical engineering.
With careful, quiet manipulation, he disengaged the first lock, allowing access to Justin's cage.

The New Balance leader stumbled out, his activist bravado in
smithereens, replaced by raw shock. His fingers wouldn't stop moving, picking at invisible threads on his makeshift clothing. "You have
no idea what they're doing down there," he whispered, eyes darting
toward the main building. "They've got... collections. Things they've
taken from us. They're studying how everything works. How *we*
work." Justin's voice broke. "I saw them with medical textbooks, taking notes. They're planning something bigger than we can imagine."

"Try," Elijah prompted, continuing work on the other locks while
watching the perimeter.

Justin's face contorted, trying to translate the abstract nightmare
into comprehensible language. "They take measurements. Record
everything. It's not just animals mimicking humans—they're trying to
understand us from the inside out." He ran trembling hands through
his filthy hair. "They took blood samples from all of us. Had medical
equipment. Knew how to use it. And those marks they're always

making? It's a language they must have just invented—I saw them teaching it to the younger ones."

As they freed the remaining people, McKenna discovered something significant inside a storage container near the cages—a small, weathered journal with faded handwriting visible on its exposed pages. The macaques must've had a reason for putting it there; it must be important. She picked it up and stashed it inside her jacket.

"We need to find Kira and Emily," she insisted once all seven Natural Balance members had been freed. "Justin, where exactly did they take them?"

The activist pointed toward a door on the station's northern wall, his hand shaking. "Through there. Down. They've got the whole place rigged with... with things they made." His voice dropped to a haunted whisper. "There was this room filled with heads. Not real ones—sculptures they made. Human faces shaped from clay and other stuff. Hundreds of them, all watching the door. And diagrams everywhere—human bodies with parts labeled by different scratch marks. They're learning us like we're a system to hack."

The door Justin indicated led to a narrow stairwell descending into darkness. Two Natural Balance members were brave or curious enough to join them, while the rest huddled above ground, melting into the tree line.

The air that wafted up from below carried a complex bouquet of smells that made them feel woozy. As they descended, the temperature dropped dramatically. The walls transitioned from wood to stone, then concrete, revealing this structure extended far deeper than any standard ranger station blueprint would indicate. The steps themselves became increasingly uneven, as though designed for creatures with different physical proportions than humans.

The stairwell opened into a space that housed a comprehensive information center with documents stamped "CLASSIFIED," technical manuals, and charts of human behavioral patterns arranged on walls and tables. But what dominated the space were artifacts constructed from scavenged materials that defied understanding.

Human-like figures stood in the center of the room, constructed from wire, plastic, and organic materials, their proportions oddly accurate. Each had been modified in ways that suggested experimentation—limbs elongated or shortened, facial features altered, internal structures visible through transparent sections. Not art but study models.

The walls bore diagrams of human anatomy, nervous systems, brain structures, annotated with the same symbolic language they'd seen. There was also small machinery constructed from electronics, chemical apparatus assembled from medical equipment and kitchen gadgets, and what seemed to be prototype weapons adapted for macaque physiology.

This wasn't just a hiding place or command center. It was a research facility dedicated to what looked to be the study of humans—their biology, psychology, and technology—by creatures who should never have possessed such capacity for abstract thought or investigation.

"They've been gathering information for years," Elijah realized, his voice sharp with growing horror. "Something like this doesn't just spring up overnight."

McKenna focused on a particular section where medical references had been gathered alongside pharmacological resources. "They're not only maintaining their enhancement; my guess is they're actively seeking to accelerate it."

Justin moved close to them. "You don't get it, do you? They're not just getting smarter—they're trying to understand how we think so they can anticipate what we'll do next. I saw them testing each other, role-playing human responses." He swallowed hard, the sound amplified in the unnatural stillness. "They're learning to think like us so they can beat us at our own game."

Their investigation was interrupted by sounds of movement from the central station area—multiple small bodies moving toward the chamber. What came for them in the darkness above wasn't just physical danger but the manifestation of intelligence without empathy, strategy without mercy, learning without wisdom. A mirror reflecting humanity's capacity for logic without the moral frameworks designed to contain it.

They couldn't sit and wait to be found. They hurried back up the crooked stairway and rejoined the freed prisoners who waited by the edge of the dense forest.

An inhuman shriek pierced the air—or more than one. The sound seemed to be coming from everywhere and nowhere, echoing through the underground chambers with a disorienting resonance. It was modulated wail that contained elements of warning, and something else: triumph. The screams rose and fell in what could only be described as a pattern, almost linguistic in its complexity.

McKenna's eyes met Elijah's, and he saw his own horror reflected there. "Damn." The curse ripped from his throat, louder than he would have liked. Their cover was blown—either they'd triggered something, or Cooper's team had already been spotted. No time for analysis now.

McKenna's face hardened. "Get them out," she ordered Justin, jerking her chin toward his shell-shocked companions. "Drainage ditch to the stream, then west. Find Cooper. Tell him we're going deeper." Two bodies moved more quietly than five. Theoretically.

Justin nodded, his earlier bravado evaporated. Amazing how imminent death clarified priorities, Elijah thought.

As the group stumbled toward escape, McKenna and Elijah slipped back toward the stairwell—the same darkness they'd just fled. The stairs betrayed them. What should have been familiar territory opened into virgin darkness, the air thick with something organic and amiss. McKenna's flashlight carved a tentative cone through the black, revealing rows of specimens that made Elijah's scientist brain stutter. Fungi sprouted from containers, some pulsing with bioluminescence that shouldn't exist in these species. The notation system—primitive but elegant—documented each experiment.

"Jesus," Elijah breathed. "They're running trials. This is systematic ethnopharmacology—controlled cultivation, documented results. They're not just using compounds, they're *creating* them."

McKenna pressed something into his palm—a journal, leather cracked with age. While she searched for any trace of Kira, Elijah angled his light across pages that made his blood chill.

*Dr. Richard Harlow, 1985.* Five years after the colony's arrival. The neat handwriting deteriorated as entries progressed, clinical observations giving way to barely controlled panic.

*"Cognitive capabilities exceed all documented parameters. Problem-solving, tool use, cooperation complexity—all accelerating. Genetic markers confirm APEX origin despite termination reports. Compound P-17 present across multiple generations via epigenetic expression. Containment protocols urgently required before acceleration becomes self-sustaining."*

The final entry twitched in fits and starts, with some passages crossed out before concluding: *"They watch me work. Not observing—learning. Replicating my methods, adapting techniques. This isn't mimicry. They anticipate standard containment procedures. Requesting immediate extraction before—"*

Nothing after that. Just blank pages that screamed their own story.

"Elijah." McKenna's voice cut through his horror. "Back here."

The door she'd found was a rudimentary hole—shortened for smaller bodies but still human-accessible.

Those distant screeches weren't distant anymore.

McKenna shone the flashlight through the opening. "Dead end," she reported, checking the final room. "We're trapped."

The other door opened before Elijah could respond. Alpha filled the frame, his presence somehow larger than his physical form suggested. Those eyes—too sentient, too knowing—swept over them with merciless assessment. Behind him, at least fifteen macaques held formation, makeshift weapons gleaming in the flashlight beams.

McKenna stepped forward, motherly instincts taking over. "Where is she? Where's Kira?"

Alpha's head tilted—a gesture so human it made Elijah's skin crawl. After a moment, the primate gestured. A subordinate vanished, returning with something that punched the air from McKenna's lungs. Elijah heard the gasp, then looked at what the monkey was holding.

Kira's scrunchie. The purple one from the security footage.

"Is she alive?" McKenna's voice cracked. "Is she hurt?"

Instead of answering, Alpha moved to a crude drawing surface covered in symbols. His fingers—too dexterous, too deliberate—added new marks. Then he looked at Elijah. Waiting.

"Communication attempt," Elijah managed. "These symbols... location markers with temporal indicators. He's showing us where they took her. But why?"

McKenna leaned closer. "These match sites all over Cypress Grove."

Alpha watched their analysis with unnerving patience, adding clarifying symbols as they worked. This wasn't conditioning or mimicry. This was *language*—raw and alien, but undeniably intentional.

More macaques entered, carrying not weapons but documents. Blueprints. Technical specifications. Alpha directed their placement with practiced efficiency, then gestured at specific sections.

"APEX infrastructure," McKenna whispered. "Original research installations. This shows an entire complex underneath the preserve—supposedly decommissioned, but..."

The blueprints revealed tunnels, laboratories, containment areas. One section labeled "Phase II Containment" drew Alpha's urgent vocalizations—sounds that transcended language to communicate pure necessity.

"He's not threatening us," Elijah realized. "He's giving us intelligence. Kira's there, and he wants us to understand why."

Alpha's nod—distinctly, disturbingly cognizant—confirmed it.

Then chaos erupted outside. Cooper's team, closing fast.

The macaques shifted instantly from interaction to evacuation mode—securing materials, implementing what looked like a well-rehearsed bugout protocol. But they weren't preparing to fight. They were ready to vanish.

Alpha approached once more, pressing tree bark into McKenna's hands. A map, crude but clear, marking the most immediate path to the underground facility.

Before they could process it fully, he indicated a concealed floor panel—an escape route. The message was unmistakable: *leave now, this way, before Cooper arrives.*

"He's helping us," McKenna breathed. "Why?"

Alpha's final gesture defied evolutionary logic. He took Harlow's journal, flipped to a hand-drawn map that matched his bark drawing, establishing the connection. Then, with movements that were practiced despite their impossibility, he mimed opening a door, touched his chest, and extended his hand toward them.

Safe passage. From one intelligence to another.

Cooper's team hit the building's perimeter. No more time. McKenna and Elijah moved as one toward the escape hatch, Alpha watching with an expression that surpassed taxonomy—understanding, purpose, and something almost like respect.

As they dropped into darkness, following a map drawn by inhuman hands toward a daughter stolen for unknowable reasons, Elijah's mind reeled. They weren't just witnessing evolution. They were negotiating with it. And somewhere in the abandoned depths of human ambition, Kira Dubrow waited at the center of an experiment that had spiraled beyond anyone's control.

# CHAPTER 13

McKenna's flashlight carved through the underground darkness like a scalpel through flesh. The beam caught on moisture-slick walls that shifted from cave to tunnel, natural formations giving way to human engineering—and then to something else. Smaller hands had been at work here too, creating passages within passages, a parasitic architecture that made her skin crawl with its scrupulous, alien precision. Tiny finger-width grooves ran along the lower portion of the walls, creating what looked like communication conduits.

The air tasted wrong. Bat guano and minerals, sure, but underneath lurked something chemical. Abandoned experiments. Failed futures. The kind of smell that belonged in nightmares about government facilities you weren't supposed to know existed—formaldehyde mixed with something metallic and bitter that coated the back of her throat, making each breath feel contaminated.

"Emergency evac route," Elijah murmured beside her, his voice doing that thing where he pretended scientific detachment could armor him against fear. She'd come to know him better than ever in these few fraught days. His knuckles were white around his own flashlight, betraying the calm in his voice. "For when things went sideways. Standard protocol in facilities of this classification."

"Or when the test subjects started thinking for themselves." McKenna kept her light steady on the wall—not random scratches but that damned symbol system that proved these creatures had language. Had culture. Had *killed*. The symbols resembled primitive pictographs combined with abstract geometric shapes, repeated with variations that suggested syntax. "They've colonized the whole network. Look at how they've modified the ventilation shafts—they've created a hierarchical structure."

McKenna's fingers traced a section where the original ventilation duct had been widened, the metal peeled back with methodical precision to create what looked like a nursery space. The walls here were lined with soft fibers—plant material, but selectively harvested and woven.

"I keep coming back to the timing," she whispered. "What if it was our construction that triggered all this? We tore up their forest, ripped into their territory with excavators and drills."

Elijah angled his light where she pointed, listening for more.

"The vibrations alone would have disrupted their established colonies." McKenna swept her beam across the floor where pale, thread-like mycelia spread in controlled patterns. "These mushrooms were more than likely planted in these caves after we drove them from their natural growing locations."

The fungi glowed with faint bioluminescence when her light passed over them, a ghostly blue-green that pulsed like a heartbeat. Some caps had been harvested, others left to mature.

"We didn't just make them angry," McKenna realized. "We forced them to act."

"We need to do the same," Elijah said grimly, moving forward. "Act."

The map Alpha had pressed into McKenna's hands—the surface scraped and stained with plant pigments to create contrast—guided them through junctions that shouldn't have made sense but did.

Twenty minutes in, her scientist brain and her mother brain were locked in a cage match. One catalogued unprecedented interspecies communication and adaptation of human infrastructure. The other screamed that her daughter was somewhere in this darkness with creatures that decorated trees with Earl Simmons' intestines and then beheaded him.

They hit a three-way split. McKenna checked the map, middle passage, when footsteps echoed behind them. Not the measured tread of Cooper's team—these were frantic, stumbling, punctuated by harsh breathing and occasional whispers.

"Dr. Dubrow?" Justin Reeves stumbled into view with three of his Natural Balance cohorts, looking like they'd been chewed up and spat out. Their macaque-made clothing was torn and filthy, and their faces were streaked with dirt and what might have been blood. "We couldn't reach the tracker. Those things were everywhere—they herded us like cattle, blocked every exit except this one."

"Those things," McKenna bit out, the words sharp with frustration and fear, "apparently know where my daughter is. And have names, species classifications, and neural structures that your group never bothered to understand before deciding to 'liberate' them."

"That map...?" Justin's eyes fixed on the bark in her hands with a mixture of horror and fascination. "They gave it to you?"

"Yes, I'm following their map. Alpha gave it to me specifically."

"You're trusting them?" Justin's voice cracked like a teenager's, his environmental righteousness evaporating in the face of reality.

"I was wrong, okay? They're not Disney animals. They're not pets. They're—"

"Intelligent beings with their own agenda," Elijah interrupted. "Their cognitive enhancement created unprecedented neural pathways. We've seen evidence of them accessing the internet."

Justin's head hung in apparent shame and contrition. "That was us. We took down the comm systems. We had people on the outside, too. Hacking social media accounts. Cutting down trees to block the roads. Natural Balance—"

McKenna turned toward the central passage, cutting him off. "They have Kira. They showed us where. Follow or don't." Her voice left no room for debate, the maternal imperative overriding any semblance of scientific curiosity and caution.

She didn't wait to see what they'd choose. Of course they followed, their footsteps reluctant but steady behind her. No one wanted to be alone in these tunnels.

The shaft widened into a manmade chamber—reinforced walls, proper floors, junction boxes for dead electrical systems. Military-grade construction that had weathered decades of neglect remarkably well. The macaques had retrofitted it all, adding their own entrances, storage spaces, and those symbols that might as well have been blaring, *We own this now*. Some areas showed evidence of purposeful modification—ventilation expanded, cables stripped and repurposed, small alcoves carved into the walls at macaque height.

They kept going.

Five minutes later, the passage opened into a chamber that stopped them cold, the beams of their flashlights crossing and illuminating something that defied immediate comprehension.

"Don't move," Elijah warned, his hand shooting out to halt their progress. "Let me analyze what we're seeing."

The display at the center wasn't accidental. Concentric circles of stolen objects—tools, electronics, medical supplies—all arranged around a plastic model of a human brain. The kind McKenna had used to teach Kira about neural structures when she was ten and still thought her mom's job was cool. Each circle tended to follow a logic—closest to the brain were devices, then tools, weapons, containers, and finally natural objects like specially selected stones and branches.

"It's a concept map," Elijah breathed, his eyes wide with fascination. "They're showing us how they categorize knowledge. The brain is the central node, everything else radiating outward by function and relationship. This is extraordinary—a physical manifestation of their cognitive taxonomy."

McKenna studied the medical supplies despite herself. Pharmaceuticals separated from surgical tools. Diagnostics distinct from treatment. They understood categories beyond 'sharp' and 'not sharp.' They'd organized antibiotics by type, arranged syringes by gauge, even separated medications in a way that suggested they understood different physiological systems.

"Why build this?" Justin whispered, his Save-the-Macaques bravado apparently having died in whatever hole they'd crawled through. He stood half-hidden behind one of his companions, eyes darting between the display and the dark tunnel mouths.

"Because they're trying to talk to us," Elijah said, crouching to examine the arrangement without disturbing it. "Establishing a framework for communication. They understand we process information differently, so they've created a visual representation of—"

Sound echoed from a side tunnel—the soft, deliberate padding of multiple feet moving in coordinated rhythm. McKenna's hand found her dart gun, fingers closing around the grip.

Justin and his crew turned tail like startled rabbits, bolting back the way they'd come, their footsteps receding rapidly into the darkness, leaving her and Elijah alone with whatever was coming.

McKenna raised her weapon, positioning herself between the approaching sounds and Elijah, who remained transfixed by the brain-centered display.

"Mom!"

The word hit McKenna like a gut-punch. Kira stood in a doorway—alive, whole, not covered in blood or missing any fingers. Behind her, juvenile macaques moved with the same care and poise as their elders.

"Kira." McKenna forced herself not to charge forward and grab her daughter. The young macaques weren't restraining her, but they weren't decoration either. "Are you hurt? Did they—"

"They didn't hurt me." Kira's face showed confusion, not trauma. Maybe a little awe. "They've been showing me things. Trying to explain."

The juveniles maintained their positions—guards or guides, McKenna couldn't tell. Probably both.

"What happened? Why did they take you?"

"Emily said they needed help." Kira's voice dropped. "Said Justin's group had made contact, that the macaques were trying to communicate about something important. Something they needed a human teenager for because of... brain development stages?"

*Jesus.* Using her daughter as a neurological Rosetta Stone.

"Where's Emily?"

"Working with older ones on plant classification. She's actually having fun. Won't shut up about ethnobotanical significance. Whatever that means."

Kira turned. "Come on, it's okay." Her voice was steady, confident in a way that McKenna found both reassuring and unsettling. How had her daughter adapted so quickly to these circumstances?

The young simians flanked her daughter, their movements synchronized yet somehow natural. They weren't restraining Kira, but their protective formation suggested both guardianship and surveillance. Their intelligent eyes scanned McKenna and Elijah continuously, assessing potential threats.

They followed Kira deeper into the facility, past corroded doors marked "Phase II Development Sector" in fading military stencil. Paint peeled away in long strips, revealing decades of neglect. The security systems had died long ago, leaving the macaques free to customize access while keeping the structural bones of the place intact. McKenna noticed claw marks where electronic locks had been dismantled, replaced with mechanisms the primates could manipulate more easily.

The laboratory beyond made McKenna's stomach drop, a visceral reaction that sent bile gurgling up her throat.

"Holy shit," she whispered, her voice barely audible even in the cavernous silence.

This portion of the compound wasn't research. This was a weapons program, plain and simple. Neural imaging systems with military designations still visible. Pharmaceutical stations with reinforced containment protocols. Monitoring equipment that belonged in a sci-fi horror movie, designed to measure combat effectiveness rather than scientific progress. The macaques had preserved it all like some twisted museum of their own creation, a testament to their origins that they'd maintained with reverence.

"Project APEX," Elijah read from protected documents encased in plastic sheeting, his academic excitement grotesquely incongruous in context. His fingers quaked slightly as he turned pages. "Directed cognitive evolution through genetic modification and neurochemical intervention. They were building battlefield assets, which we suspected. But this confirms it."

"They want us to know what was done to them," McKenna realized, scanning the meticulously preserved equipment. "Military experiments. Enhanced problem-solving for combat applications. They're showing us their origin story."

"Phase II was worse." Elijah's face had gone pale, the blood draining visibly as he continued reading. "Transgenerational enhancement. Epigenetic modifications designed to compound across breeding cycles. Progressive evolution, accelerating with each generation. They weren't just creating enhanced individuals—they were engineering an entirely new species trajectory."

"Supposedly terminated in '79," he continued, flipping through yellowed documentation with increasing agitation. "All subjects to be euthanized, research discontinued. Except—"

"Except they sold them to a movie production." McKenna's dark humor kicked in, the only defense against the horror of it. Her laugh was brittle, fracturing in the sterile air. "Nothing says 'ethical oversight' like turning your failed super-soldiers into Hollywood extras. Christ, the military industrial complex at its finest."

"They're scared, Mom."

Kira's words cut through McKenna's bitter spiral, bringing her back into the conversation. "Scared? They've killed people, Kira. They've turned Cypress Grove into—" she gestured helplessly, unable to find words adequate to describe the carnage they'd witnessed.

"Not frightened-scared. Strategic-scared." Her daughter had that teenage gift for cutting through bullshit, seeing patterns adults often missed. "They showed me videos, news clips, military footage. They know what humans do to threats. They found this place, figured out what they are, and realized we'd destroy them if we knew. They've been studying us as much as we've been studying them."

"Preemptive self-defense," Elijah translated, his academic detachment returning as he processed this information. "They recognized their evolution would trigger termination protocols. They acted before we could." His fingers tapped nervously against the folder he held, a rhythmic counterpoint to the silence.

McKenna watched her daughter standing nonchalantly among creatures that could tear her apart, speaking for beings that may not be monsters after all. Or might be precisely the monsters humans had *made* them to be. The contradiction twisted in her gut.

"Maximum Acceptable Parameters." Elijah held up a folder that might as well have been marked 'Death Warrant,' its military classification stamps still visible through decades of discoloration. "They've exceeded every threshold for elimination. According to these guidelines, they shouldn't be here."

The juveniles shifted uneasily, their movements creating a ripple effect through the room, and Alpha entered through a side door. Of course he'd been watching. Testing. The scarred bastard had led her here not out of kindness but calculation, every step a measured risk assessment.

The macaque extended his hand—human gesture, inhuman strength barely contained beneath his matted fur. The thing that had orchestrated a siege, killed her neighbors, taken her daughter, wanted to shake hands. The absurdity would have been comical in any other context.

McKenna took it. His grip was controlled, precise, warm. Another data point in whatever assessment he was running. She felt the healing cut on his palm, rough with scabs. She also felt herself being measured, evaluated against criteria she couldn't begin to understand.

"What now?" she asked the charged air between them. "Cypress Grove is under siege. People are dying. Eventually, someone's going to call in an airstrike. This doesn't end well for anyone."

Alpha moved with deliberate purpose to a territorial map spread across a nearby table, indicating boundaries with precision. The preserve. The town. A line drawn between them with what looked like charcoal.

"Territorial division," Elijah interpreted, leaning forward to get a better look. "Separate but—"

"Not separate." Kira stepped forward, her confidence growing. "Some contact. They don't want to be cut off from us. They want... a truce, maybe?"

Alpha added documents about research continuation, spreading them beside the map. Structured observation. Then pointed at McKenna and Elijah specifically, his gaze fixed on them with unnerving intensity.

"He wants us as intermediaries." McKenna took a beat. "Scientific observers managing human-macaque interaction. Ambassadors to a species we created but don't understand."

The opportunity was staggering in its scientific implications. The impossibility, more so. Convincing anyone that enhanced murder-macaques deserved study instead of extermination? That ship had sailed when they started using human organs as Christmas decorations. The military would never allow this experiment to continue once they understood what was happening.

"We need to talk to Harding and Holden," she said, pragmatism winning over everything else. "Before someone decides to napalm the whole preserve. They need to understand what we're dealing with."

Alpha's vocalizations—a complex series of sounds that were almost language-like—sent his subordinates into immediate motion. They gathered maps, communication devices, what looked like signal equipment, preparing for something.

"Escort protocols," Elijah observed as he watched the macaques work. "They're giving us safe passage back. Fascinating how they've adapted human security procedures."

McKenna turned to her daughter. "You're really okay? They didn't hurt you at all?"

Kira nodded, her expression earnest. "They were careful with me. Gentle, even. They just needed someone to understand. Someone whose brain was still flexible enough to grasp how they think."

"And do you?" McKenna searched her daughter's face for signs of coercion or Stockholm syndrome.

"Yeah." Her daughter's insight hit harder than any academic analysis could have. "They're terrified we'll kill them for becoming what we made them to be. Wouldn't you be?"

As they prepared to leave, Elijah gathered documents that would either save or damn them all, meticulously organizing papers that represented the culmination of years of research gone catastrophically wrong. First contact with intelligence they'd created but couldn't control—a watershed moment in scientific history that no ethics committee had ever prepared protocols for. Evolution at gunpoint.

"You realize what this is?" Elijah murmured as Alpha organized their exit.

"The beginning of a beautiful friendship?" McKenna's dark humor was all she had left, the gallows wit that had gotten her through countless crises—mundane compared to this—surfacing now when she needed it most. "Or the prologue to *Planet of the Apes, Florida*

*Edition.* Complete with swamp tours and souvenir t-shirts." The joke fell flat even to her own ears, but it kept the panic at bay.

Alpha led them toward daylight, every calculated movement a reminder that understanding didn't equal safety. His posture spoke volumes—alert, protective, but with an underlying wariness that suggested he trusted them only as far as his enhanced cognitive abilities could predict their behavior. These weren't just smart animals. They were weaponized intelligence wrapped in fur and fury, their ethical framework as alien as their enhanced cognition was familiar.

Whether Cypress Grove would survive its unintended first contact remained to be seen. The preserve had become ground zero for a new kind of intelligence, one that might eventually challenge humanity's dominance. But as they climbed toward a surface that would never feel quite safe again, McKenna knew one thing with bone-deep certainty: They'd created their own monsters through hubris and military funding. Now everyone would have to live with the consequences.

Alpha's milky eye caught the light as they climbed, a ghostly reminder that some experiments couldn't be contained, some evolution couldn't be stopped, and some mistakes came with teeth. That damaged eye, evidence of his survival against all odds, seemed to reflect back all their scientific arrogance and shortsightedness.

# CHAPTER 14

S heriff Lucas Harding wiped blood from a cut above his eye, the adrenaline spike having numbed him to the injury sustained during the macaques' most recent assault on the high school shelter.

The gymnasium had been transformed from emergency command center to field hospital, with Dr. Thatcher and Vivian Santos directing civilian volunteers in treating the wounded. Twenty-three injuries in the past four hours alone, ranging from minor lacerations to critical cases requiring emergency surgery with severely limited supplies.

"Sheriff," Deputy Miller approached, his clothes torn from the frontline defense efforts. "Perimeter Team Alpha reports the eastern approach has been secured again, but they're using different tactics now—sudden burst attacks rather than sustained pressure."

Harding nodded grimly, recognizing the strategy. "They're conserving resources while mapping our defensive capabilities. Preparing for a coordinated assault once they've identified optimal breach points."

"There's more," Miller continued. "The spotters report significant movement in the forest north of town. Large numbers gathering, appearing to organize into operational units. Cooper estimates at least one hundred fifty visible, with more likely concealed in heavier vegetation."

The implications settled heavily on Harding's shoulders. There were even more macaques than previously thought, and they were preparing a major offensive—quite possibly their final push to overwhelm the town's remaining defenses.

"What about McKenna's search team?" he asked, though he anticipated the answer.

"No contact since they entered the underground facility Cooper's team located," Miller reported. "We've maintained the designated rally point, but with communications down and increasing macaque activity in the area, extraction options are limited."

Harding checked his watch—nearly six hours since McKenna and Elijah had pursued the lead on Kira's location, following the rough map provided by the macaque leader. The probability of their safe return dwindled with each passing hour, a harsh statistical reality his law enforcement experience wouldn't allow him to ignore despite his personal hope.

Mayor Holden approached from the medical station, her hair pulled back carelessly, designer duds replaced with donated jeans and a faded Cypress Grove High sweatshirt. "The state wildlife response team finally arrived," she said, keeping her voice low to avoid alarming nearby civilians. "Regional directors Jenkins and Morales, with eight specialists. They're setting up at the eastern perimeter and going over our situation reports."

"About damn time," Harding muttered, though he recognized the response had come faster than typical bureaucracy would allow. "What resources did they bring?"

"Tranquilizer systems, capture equipment, and—" she hesitated before continuing, "—lethal options for colony eradication if containment fails."

Harding took it all in with the expression of a man watching his town circle the drain. The state had given them the green light to kill every last macaque if they couldn't get them under control—standard operating procedure for dangerous invasive species, which would've been fine if they were dealing with pythons or murder hornets instead of primates that could probably file their own tax returns. The whole "shoot first, ask questions never" approach felt like bringing a sledgehammer to brain surgery, especially now that they knew what they were really dealing with.

"Brief them on everything we've documented about tactical capabilities and coordinated operations," he instructed. "Make sure they understand we're not dealing with standard wildlife behavior patterns."

As Mayor Holden left to coordinate with the state response team, Vivian approached from the medical station, her surgical scrubs stained with blood, but her manner remained professional, despite the chaos surrounding them.

"Sheriff, I've been analyzing tissue samples from the macaque autopsy," she began, producing a tablet. "The data suggests a potential physiological vulnerability we might be able to use."

Harding's analytical mind immediately engaged with this new information. "What kind of vulnerability?"

"Their enhanced cognitive function appears linked to elevated neurochemical activity requiring specific compounds," Vivian explained, indicating complex molecular structures on the display. "The fungal matter we identified in the digestive tract contains precursors that support this enhanced neural processing. Without regular consumption, their system would experience significant neurotransmitter disruption—potentially reverting to standard macaque cognitive function over time."

"You're saying we could reverse their intelligence enhancement by cutting off access to these mushrooms?" Harding clarified, immediately recognizing the implications.

"Theoretically, yes," Vivian confirmed. "But we'd have to try it before knowing if it really works like I think it will. And they were enhanced by other means as well, so... No guarantees."

Before Harding could chase that thought any further, all hell broke loose at the east entrance. Deputies stationed there had weapons raised toward approaching figures emerging from the tree line—human figures moving with that particular shuffle of people who weren't sure if they were about to get a welcome party or a firing squad.

"Hold fire!" Harding commanded, moving rapidly toward the entrance, hand on his sidearm. "Identification protocols!"

Through his binoculars, he recognized the lead figure with a surge of relief that temporarily overwhelmed him—McKenna Dubrow, followed by Elijah Jackson and several others, including Kira. Walking. Breathing. Not being carried in pieces.

"Friendlies approaching eastern entrance," he announced over the radio network. "Maintain perimeter coverage but hold positions. Medical team to entrance for assessment."

The reunion at the perimeter checkpoint carried the awkward intensity of those who had faced death separately and returned changed by their experiences. McKenna held Kira's hand with fierce maternal protection, her knuckles tight, eyes constantly scanning her daughter's face for any sign of trauma or distress. Every few seconds, she'd pull Kira closer, as if reassuring herself that the solid warmth of her child wasn't some desperate hallucination conjured by a grieving mind.

Elijah maintained his composure despite evident shock. His shirt was untucked, mud-spattered khakis were torn at one knee, and stubble darkened his jaw. File folders were clutched in his hand like a lifeline. The scientist's eyes darted between McKenna and the security perimeter, his expression betraying the internal struggle between academic fascination and the life-threatening terror he'd just survived.

Behind them, Justin Reeves and the other Natural Balance members trudged forward with the hollow-eyed shock of civilians who had witnessed combat conditions without preparation or training. Their once-passionate environmental activism had been stripped of its ideological armor, replaced by the thousand-yard stare of those who had glimpsed nature's capacity for violence. Justin's hands were clenched, his self-righteous cockiness visibly shattered by whatever horrors they'd witnessed in compound. The conspicuous absence of Emily among their group cast a palpable shadow over their return, a void no one was ready to acknowledge aloud.

"McKenna," Harding acknowledged, relief coloring his tone. "And Kira, thank God."

"We found the underground research facility," McKenna said in a monotone. "It's the origin point of the macaques' cognitive enhancement—APEX. But the subjects were sold to that film production company instead of being euthanized, then abandoned here when the project failed. The monkeys weren't imported from the Philippines."

Harding processed this information, then said, "Inside. Dr. Santos has made a related discovery you need to hear."

As they moved through the gymnasium-turned-shelter, Harding noted the impact of their return on civilian morale—visible relief at McKenna's reappearance, hopeful whispers at Kira's safe recovery, renewed assurance in leadership continuity during crisis. These psychological factors carried tangible operational value in sustaining community resilience—a reality his military experience had impressed upon him long before he became Sheriff.

The command team huddled around the largest table like survivors around a fire—Harding, McKenna, Elijah, Vivian, Mayor Holden, Cooper, and the newly arrived state wildlife officials who still reeked of bureaucracy and disbelief. Justin lurked at the edges, his former environmental crusader confidence wiped away by the shell-shocked stare of someone whose worldview had been systematically dismantled by small, nimble hands.

Harding watched as McKenna and Elijah laid out their discoveries as if they were crime scene evidence. The underground APEX facility. Military enhancement research that should have stayed buried. Evidence of progressive cognitive evolution across generations. And Alpha—dear God, Alpha and his unsettling ability to communicate.

"They're not just smart animals anymore," McKenna said, exhaustion bleeding through her tone. "They're something entirely new. Macaque intelligence pumped full of human intervention, now evolving on its own timeline."

Elijah nodded, spreading facility documents across the table. "This isn't just targeted aggression or accelerated intellect. They're protecting themselves from what they see as an existential threat. Everything they've done to Cypress Grove is to save themselves."

Regional Director Jenkins—a man whose craggy face suggested he'd wrestled more wildlife than paperwork—studied the evidence with the skepticism of someone who'd seen too many academic theories crumble in the field. "You're asking us to treat these animals like some kind of non-human intelligence rather than dangerous pests?"

"The evidence doesn't lie," Elijah replied, cutting through the room's tension. "Their tactical operations, transmission systems, technological understanding—it all points to intelligence that functions differently than ours but meets every criterion for rational thought."

Director Morales, younger but carrying the focused intensity of someone trained for disasters, reviewed their reports with growing alarm. "Intelligence or not, they're a threat to human safety. Standard protocols exist for a reason—containment or elimination."

Vivian stepped forward, her analysis clutched like a lifeline. "Much of their enhanced cognition depends on specific compounds from local fungi. Cut off their supply, and theoretically, their capabilities diminish over generations."

"Generations?" Morales echoed. "What do we do in the meantime?"

"Containment first," McKenna suggested. "And then…"

Harding absorbed the competing perspectives, the sheriff's shrewd mind was already gaming out scenarios. Lives hung in the balance of every decision, and sunset was approaching like an execution date. "Two hours until dark," he announced, anchoring them to reality. "Intelligence says they're massing for a major assault on our shelters. Whatever we decide, it needs to happen now."

Mayor Holden leaned forward, grasping at familiar solutions. "The state team brought those specialized tranquilizer systems we discussed. Mass primate operations, non-lethal takedown—"

"Mayor," Cooper interrupted, his voice carrying the gravitas of hard-won experience, "we've been over this. These things will dismantle every conventional approach we know. Tranquilizers, barriers, standard containment—they'd see it all coming and adapt in real time. We might as well be throwing rocks at fighter jets."

Justin's voice weaseled through the air from the periphery. "I spent years fighting for animal rights. Believed we should respect their autonomy." He gestured helplessly at the documentation. "But what I saw at that station... it wasn't natural behavior. Human-like planning without human feelings. They stripped us, both figuratively and literally. More people are going to die if we don't stop them."

The admission hit like a physical blow. If even Justin—animal rights crusader extraordinaire—was advocating for action, they'd crossed into territory none of them had mapped.

"There has to be another way," McKenna insisted. "These macaques exist because of our military research. We created this situation. We owe it to everyone—human and macaque—to find a solution that doesn't end in genocide."

Kira, who'd been quietly absorbing the adult panic around her, suddenly straightened. "I can talk to them."

Every head turned. The teenager shifted under the scrutiny but held her ground with typical adolescent stubbornness mixed with unfiltered insight.

"Not talk-talk," she clarified, gaining confidence. "But they showed me their communication thing. It's like... patterns. Objects arranged in certain ways, gestures with sounds, and marks that mean stuff. The younger ones, especially—they're way more flexible than the adults. Less stuck in the whole 'humans are enemies' mindset."

Elijah studied her with scientific fascination. "Adolescent neuroplasticity. Your brain's still adaptable enough to recognize novel patterns that adult neural pathways might reject."

Harding felt a strategy crystallizing, born from desperation and impossible circumstances. "Could you actually negotiate with them? Establish real connection and understanding?"

"Maybe," Kira said honestly. "The little ones seemed interested in trying to understand me. They're not as... like I said, I don't know, as set on seeing us as threats."

Harding turned to the topographical map as disparate elements fell into place, forming a coherent plan. "What if we combine everything? Vivian's compound research gives us leverage. The facility documentation proves they fear termination protocols. Kira's established basic communication with the younger generation."

His finger traced the preserve boundaries. "We create a protected zone around the research facility and fungal growth areas. Territorial boundaries with monitoring stations. A research preserve where their development can be studied under controlled conditions."

"A reservation for monkeys," Jenkins said flatly.

"A research facility," McKenna corrected. "Where we can study this cognitive evolution while maintaining containment. Strong electric fences to keep them in but with enough room for them to feel free."

"Alpha already suggested something similar," Elijah added, producing the crude map they'd recovered. "Territorial division with interaction zones. They want security for their development, not isolation."

Director Morales assessed the proposal with professional consideration. "Resources required would be massive. Federal support, perimeter security, research infrastructure. This goes way beyond state jurisdiction."

"The scientific value justifies the investment," Elijah argued. "We're witnessing real-time cognitive evolution along non-human pathways. The applications span neuroscience to AI development."

"First, we survive the night," Harding reminded them, reality reasserting itself. "From what you've shown us here, they're preparing for a major offensive. We need a defense that protects civilians while keeping the door open for non-lethal resolution. But if that fails, all bets are off."

The planning session went on. Vivian and Elijah worked on compounds that could temporarily suppress cognitive enhancement without permanent damage—demonstration rather than implementation. McKenna and Kira created communication materials using observed symbolic systems, building bridges across species barriers. The state team integrated specialized equipment into defensive perimeters, maintaining lethal options as a final backup.

Harding coordinated everything with the methodical precision that had kept him alive through military service and law enforcement crises. Resource deployment, civilian protection, and creating space for negotiation while preparing for war.

As sunset approached, he briefed the assembled teams. "Defensive positions only," he instructed. "No offensive operations without direct authorization. Our goal is protecting civilians while creating negotiation opportunities through Kira and the research team."

The state specialists exchanged skeptical glances. Their training focused on standard wildlife protocols, not cross-species diplomacy. But Harding's authority carried weight here.

"I know this contradicts standard procedures," he acknowledged. "But we're facing something without precedent. Standard responses have failed to keep pace with their adaptive capabilities. We need innovative integration."

McKenna approached him as teams dispersed, scientific focus warring with parental terror. "Kira's our best chance, but putting her on the front lines..."

"Maximum security protocols," Harding assured her. "Cooper's identified an interaction zone with natural barriers. State specialists will maintain perimeter security with non-lethal deterrents."

McKenna nodded. "She understands their communication better than anyone. If there's any chance of resolution without extermination, it runs through her."

Darkness settled over Cypress Grove like a held breath. Final defensive preparations proceeded—position assignments, evacuation routes, medical stations ready for casualties. Each element checked and rechecked because there wouldn't be second chances.

From the eastern perimeter, Harding watched shadows move in the forest with deliberate purpose. Director Jenkins joined him with field binoculars. "Still think negotiation's viable?"

"I hope so. But they keep surprising us."

"And if all this fails?"

"Then we implement lethal force," Harding confirmed. "But we owe both species an attempt at resolution before extermination."

Cypress Grove held still as full darkness arrived. Citizens huddled in shelters, medical teams prepared for casualties, defensive units maintained vigilant perimeter watch. In the surrounding forest, macaques gathered with enhanced cognition directing sophisticated operations toward objectives only they fully understood.

Between these opposing forces, everything came down to a sixteen-year-old girl who'd stumbled into becoming humanity's translator. Kira Dubrow—more comfortable with TikTok than tactical operations—now carried the burden of potential genocide or coexistence on her shoulders. Her young brain's developing patterns might be the only thing standing between species warfare and something resembling peace.

8:47 PM. Harding's watch ticked toward the window they'd calculated—macaque assault expected between 10:00 PM and midnight, when complete darkness gave them every advantage. The communication attempt at 9:30 PM represented their last gambit before everything devolved into survival mode.

Harding shelved the philosophical weight crushing down on all of them. Right now, his job was keeping people alive. If teenage diplomacy worked, they'd have time later to process the implications. If it failed, he'd pull every trigger necessary to protect his community, no matter how intelligent the targets.

Moonlight painted the contested ground in silver and shadow. In the command center, final preparations moved with desperate efficiency. In the forest, enhanced predators positioned for war.

The military's abandoned experiment had finally reached its conclusion—cooperation or annihilation between two forms of intelligence that should never have shared the same evolutionary timeline.

The next few hours would decide which species walked away.

# CHAPTER 15

S heriff Lucas Harding crouched at the eastern perimeter, the night vision scope painting the world in sickly green phosphorescence. Seventy yards away, the negotiation zone waited like a stage set for humanity's most desperate performance. McKenna's team had arranged it meticulously—objects positioned according to macaque communication patterns, lighting that split the difference between human limitations and superior primate vision, weapons hidden but ready should diplomacy collapse into bloodshed.

Every bone in Harding's body screamed that this was suicide. The clearing offered about as much cover as a parking lot, with retreat options that could charitably be called "nonexistent." Above them, the canopy provided a highway system for creatures designed to move through trees faster than humans could run on flat ground. His response teams crouched at calculated intervals, but their training manuals had never covered "coordinated assault by cognitively enhanced primates with strategic planning capabilities."

The absurdity of the situation almost made him laugh. Almost. Because somewhere in that forest, animals were implementing battle plans that would make a Marine Corps tactician proud. And here he was, about to send a young girl to negotiate with them using finger paintings and strategic rock placement.

But conventional wisdom had taken a beating this week. Every established protocol, every "animals behave predictably" assumption, every containment method in the book—Alpha's forces had dismantled them all with the casual efficiency of chess masters playing against toddlers. When the rulebook becomes kindling, you write new rules or you die by the old ones. Traditional approaches had earned them a body count and a besieged town. Time to try something that would either make history or end it.

"Team positions confirmed," Deputy Miller reported through the radio network. "Perimeter security established at all designated points. Medical response on standby at rally point Charlie."

"Copy that," Harding acknowledged. "Maintain alert status and communication discipline. No engagement without direct authorization, regardless of macaque movement patterns."

He checked his watch—9:28 PM. The team would leave the shelter perimeter any minute. McKenna, Elijah, and Kira would go into the clearing carrying specific objects they believed would help with communication, while state wildlife specialists maintained defensive positioning at established perimeter points.

Director Jenkins materialized beside him like a ghost in military gear, his substantial frame moving with the unnerving silence of someone who'd spent many years hunting things that could hunt back. "Last chance to pull the plug, Sheriff. We've got enough tranquilizer capacity to drop every monkey in a five-mile radius. Say the word, and we end this the old-fashioned way."

Harding could appreciate Jenkins' position—the man had built his career on proven methodologies, decades of fieldwork that said "dangerous animals get contained or eliminated, period." In Jenkins' world, protocols existed because they worked, and deviation meant body bags.

"Those protocols assume we're dealing with animals," Harding replied, watching shadows flicker at the forest edge with movements too coordinated for comfort. "These things have turned every conventional approach into a learning exercise. They study our tactics, adapt in real-time, then use our own methods against us."

Jenkins' reluctant nod gave the air of professional defeat. "Teams are locked and loaded for immediate deployment. But I'm putting it on record—sending civilians into a potential kill zone for an experiment with about as much chance of success as a snowball in hell."

"Duly noted," Harding said, respecting the man's honesty while accepting the crushing weight of command. Sometimes you had to choose between bad options and worse ones.

The sheriff's radio crackled to life—McKenna's voice steady as surgical steel, though he could hear the mother's terror bleeding through the professional facade. "Command, negotiation team ready for deployment. Requesting final authorization."

Harding drew a breath that tasted like gunpowder and desperation. In thirty seconds, he'd either make history or become a cautionary tale about the dangers of thinking outside the box when the box contained apex predators with human-level intelligence.

"Authorization confirmed. Proceed as planned. All security teams—defensive positions only. Nobody fires without my direct order."

Through the green-tinted scope, he watched three figures emerge from the shelter's safety like sacrificial offerings walking toward an altar. McKenna moved with clinical confidence, Elijah clutched his documentation like a shield made of paper, and between them, Kira carried humanity's last desperate attempt at conversation.

They looked impossibly small against the vast darkness ahead, three people walking into territory ruled by creatures that had rewritten the laws of evolution through sheer, terrifying intelligence.

"Movement, northwest quadrant," Cooper's voice crackled through the radio like a death knell. "Fifteen subjects in the trees, thirty yards out. They're watching."

Harding adjusted his scope, finding the macaques positioned with perfect observation angles, clear escape routes, overlapping fields of fire. If he'd been planning this himself, he couldn't have done it better. The realization sent ice through his veins.

In the clearing, the negotiation team moved like actors hitting their marks on a stage lit by floodlights and moonlight. McKenna faced the most likely approach vector with the calm of a surgeon preparing for a difficult operation. Elijah spread his papers like tarot cards that might predict the future. Kira arranged her collection of symbolic objects with the focused intensity of someone building a bridge between worlds using pocket change and hope.

Minutes crawled by. The forest canopy rustled with deliberate movement—not random animal activity but coordinated repositioning. The macaques were studying every angle, every vulnerability, mapping human behavior patterns before committing to contact.

Then the shadows at the clearing's edge shifted with purpose rather than caution.

Alpha stepped into moonlight like a nightmare given form, his good amber eye catching the light in ways that made Harding's trigger finger itch. The macaque leader stood at the forest boundary, evaluating their desperate diplomatic offering with the appraising look of a general surveying enemy positions.

*Here we go*, Harding thought. "Primary subject identified northern perimeter," he reported to all security teams. "Maintain positions and alert status. No engagement without direct authorization."

Alpha stayed at the forest edge for nearly three minutes, assessing the clearing arrangement with evident consideration. Finally, he made his decision, stepping from the cover into the clearing with extreme caution. Six macaques accompanied him in protective formation—larger males carrying tools that could function as weapons if necessary. Their approach maintained distance while establishing a direct line of sight to the human negotiation team, standard positioning for uncertain engagement scenarios.

Kira broke the frozen tableau first, stepping forward despite her mother's reflexive grab for her arm. The teenager moved with the peculiar fearlessness that only comes from not quite grasping the full horror of your situation. She knelt beside her arrangement of objects—stones, sticks, bits of metal—and began adjusting them with the focused intensity of someone defusing a bomb with origami instructions.

Alpha's scarred head tilted, studying her movements with an astuteness that made Harding's skin crawl. The creature's posture shifted from predatory readiness to something that might have been curiosity if you could forget the razor-sharp canines and the way his good eye tracked every micro-movement like a sniper acquiring targets. When Alpha gestured to his security team, the subtle relaxation in their aggressive stance felt less like peace and more like a cat deciding not to pounce—yet.

"Movement detected across all perimeter sectors," Cooper's voice crackled through the radio, each word dropping the temperature another degree. "Multiple groups establishing observation positions with sightlines to the clearing. Current count exceeds fifty individuals in tactical formation."

Fifty. Harding's throat went dry. They'd walked into the center of a living trap, surrounded by creatures intelligent enough to coordinate complex operations but still fundamentally predators who could rip a human apart with their bare hands.

In the clearing, Alpha approached Kira's arrangement like a chess master considering his next move. He examined each element with the methodical attention of someone reading a language written in blood and bone. Then he began adding his own pieces to the puzzle—papers from the facility, basic maps, and most unnervingly, what looked like carefully preserved fungal specimens that gleamed wetly in the moonlight.

"They're attempting reciprocal communication," Elijah's voice came through the radio, his academic detachment a thin veneer over what had to be bone-deep terror. "Alpha is implementing symbolic exchange. The arrangement appears to reference territorial boundaries and resource access protocols."

Kira responded with the adaptability of youth, incorporating Alpha's contributions while adding new elements of her own. Watching them work together—human teenager and enhanced predator—felt like witnessing something that violated the natural order. This shouldn't be possible. Shouldn't be happening. Yet here they were, two different species developing a shared language in real time while surrounded by enough firepower to level a city block.

The symbolic negotiation continued building complexity like a fever dream gaining momentum. Each exchange added new layers of meaning, new possibilities for common rapport across an evolutionary divide that should have been unbridgeable. Harding found himself holding his breath, watching history unfold or disaster crystallize—impossible to tell which.

Then the forest shifted.

"Something's wrong," Cooper's voice cut through the radio static with the sharp edge of a man who'd just spotted his own death approaching. "The southern macaque teams are implementing what looks like assault preparation rather than security positioning. Movement patterns don't match Alpha's standard protocols."

The night air suddenly felt thinner, charged with the electricity that comes just before lightning strikes. Through his scope, Harding could see the discipline fracturing—some macaque units maintaining their observation posts while others moved with different intent entirely. The unified command structure they'd observed was splintering, and in that fracture, violence waited like a loaded gun with a hair trigger.

Harding's scope revealed the nightmare unfolding in real time—fifteen macaques breaking from the disciplined formations like cancer cells escaping containment. These weren't following Alpha's methodical chess-master approach. They moved with the chaotic hunger of predators who'd finally decided to stop playing with their food.

The realization hit him like ice water: Alpha wasn't in complete control. There were factions. Disagreement. And the disagreement was about whether humans deserved to live through the night.

The splinter group erupted from the southern tree line with terrifying ease, brandishing improvised weapons that gleamed in the moonlight. Sharpened sticks, modified tools, fragments of metal that had been honed to points. This wasn't animal aggression—it was calculated violence with the efficiency of an abattoir.

"Hostile movement south quadrant," Harding barked into his radio, his voice cutting through the night like a blade. "Security teams

Delta and Echo—engage with non-lethal deterrents. All other teams maintain perimeter containment."

The air filled with the compressed hiss of deterrent systems deploying—impact-activated irritants designed to send normal primates fleeing in chemical-induced panic. For a moment, hope flickered as the defensive barrier materialized between the attackers and the clearing.

Then the macaques proved once again that standard rules no longer applied.

Instead of dispersing, they split into coordinated sub-units with the fluid precision of special forces. Some neutralized the deterrent launchers with surgical strikes, while others advanced through calculated vectors that minimized exposure. They'd studied human defensive systems, learned their weaknesses, and developed countermeasures that turned non-lethal deterrents into expensive paperweights.

"Deterrents ineffective," Deputy Miller's voice carried the controlled panic of someone watching their carefully planned defenses crumble in real time. "Hostile subjects continuing approach with counter-measures. Permission to implement secondary response protocol."

"Affirmative," Harding authorized, the word tasting like copper in his mouth. "Secondary response authorized in south and southeast quadrants only. Maintain containment perimeter—priority on negotiation team protection."

The net launchers deployed, specialized systems designed to entangle aggressive primates without permanent harm. A few of the attackers went down in synthetic webbing, but the others adapted instantly, their enhanced intelligence turning each captured comrade into a lesson learned rather than a victory achieved.

But then something happened that redefined everything Harding thought he understood about their situation.

Alpha didn't join the assault. He didn't withdraw. Instead, the scarred leader implemented immediate defensive positioning around Kira and the communication arrangement, his sharp vocalizations cutting through the chaos like orders barked on a battlefield. His security team wheeled to face the approaching hostiles rather than the humans, creating a living shield between the attackers and their negotiators.

"Alpha's group is protecting the negotiation team," Elijah's voice came through the radio with the stunned wonder of someone watching the laws of nature rewrite themselves. "This appears to be internal conflict rather than coordinated assault—a splinter faction acting against Alpha's operational directives."

The implications crashed over Harding like a cold wave. They weren't facing a unified enemy. They were witnessing a civil war fought with claws and brains between two visions of what these enhanced creatures should become. And somehow, impossibly, a teenage girl had become the focal point around which the future of two species would be decided.

In the clearing, surrounded by predators choosing sides in a conflict that could end with her torn apart or elevated to something like sainthood, Kira continued arranging her objects with the determined focus of someone who understood that her next move might be humanity's last.

# CHAPTER 16

The ferocious macaques hit the clearing's edge like a wave of calculated wrath, their sophisticated understanding of human defensive capabilities evident in every movement. They'd studied the security teams, learned the patterns, and now they exploited every weakness. As they prepared for their final assault, Alpha did something that redefined everything Harding thought he understood about leadership.

Instead of withdrawal or defensive positioning, Alpha launched himself directly at the attacking faction. His security squad moved like a machine, creating a protective perimeter around the negotiation team while their leader advanced on what appeared to be the splinter group's commander with the focused intensity of a missile seeking its target.

"Primary hostile identified," Cooper's voice cut through the radio static with professional clarity. "Large male, distinctive chest and back scarring, missing portion of right ear. Directing assault operations through gesture system similar to Alpha's but with variant patterns."

Through his scope, Harding watched the creature Cooper had spotted—a particularly massive specimen whose skin bore scars like battle medals and whose damaged ear gave him a permanently aggressive expression. Unlike Alpha's controlled, game-master movements, this individual radiated pure violence barely contained by intelligence. His gestures carried the same structural elements as Alpha's system, but implemented with sharp, staccato movements that suggested a fundamentally different philosophy: might makes right, and negotiations were for the weak.

"I'm designating the splinter leader as 'Scarback' for tactical identification," Harding instructed his teams, the name fitting like a glove on something designed to inflict damage. "All teams maintain current engagement parameters. Lethal options remain unauthorized except for immediate life threat to civilians."

Throughout the surrounding forest, macaques visibly chose sides, some maintaining security positions while others engaged in direct combat that lit up multiple perimeter points like fireworks made of flesh and fury.

In the clearing's center, McKenna had pulled Kira close while Elijah continued documenting everything with the focus of someone who understood they were witnessing scientific history being written in blood. Alpha's security maintained their protective formation around the humans, engaging attacking macaques with coordinated efficiency that would have impressed a Marine drill instructor, while their leader stalked toward his confrontation with Scarback, long fangs bared.

"Sheriff," McKenna's voice came through the radio. "We need to maintain the negotiation framework despite the conflict. Kira believes Alpha is defending the contact attempt against internal opposition."

"Understood," Harding acknowledged. "Security teams will support defensive positioning around the negotiation team while avoiding engagement with Alpha's faction. Director Jenkins, maintain your specialized teams in containment posture focused on the hostile faction only."

As security forces implemented these surreal adjusted parameters—fighting alongside some enhanced predators while containing others—the confrontation between Alpha and Scarback reached its inevitable climax at the clearing's southern edge. The two macaque leaders faced each other in a dominance challenge, posturing that spoke to millions of years of evolutionary programming. Their vocalizations carried content that transcended human understanding but conveyed unmistakable meaning: only one would walk away as leader.

The macaques circled each other with calculated positioning, each assessing their physical capabilities and vulnerabilities before engagement, much like generals studying battlefield maps. Their movements demonstrated methodical thinking about approach vectors, defensive positioning, and strike opportunities—primate strength and aggression directed by strategic temperance that was at odds with their natural instincts.

The two macaques engaged with brutal efficiency that utilized every natural weapon evolution had provided—teeth designed to crush bone, claws that could open arteries, powerful limbs that could shatter skulls—all deployed with precision targeting of vital areas. Alpha's approach favored calculated strikes that minimized counter-attack exposure, while Scarback went with overwhelming force patterns that prioritized devastating damage over anything else.

From his position, Harding caught movement in his peripheral vision—Cooper discreetly adjusting his rifle, establishing clear lines of sight to both battling leaders. The hunter's assessment had identified an opportunity to decapitate the macaque command structure with two well-placed shots, potentially creating operational chaos that would allow conventional containment to succeed where negotiation might fail.

Before Harding could issue orders through the radio, McKenna acted with decisiveness that surprised him. She moved from her protective position near Kira, deliberately placing herself in Cooper's firing line while making direct eye contact with the hunter. No words were needed—her intention registered clearly as a choice between diplomatic resolution and practical intervention that would destroy any chance of coexistence.

Cooper held position for several heartbeats that felt like hours before reluctantly lowering his weapon in acknowledgment of command authority. His assessment wasn't wrong—eliminating both faction leaders would likely create operational chaos, potentially allowing conventional methods to succeed where they had consistently failed. But such intervention would also obliterate the negotiation opportunity Alpha's faction had risked everything to create, condemning both species to continued conflict rather than potential coexistence.

The combat between Alpha and Scarback escalated to a ferocious crescendo. Each macaque moved with a lethal grace, their bodies a blur of primal strength and strategic precision. The air was thick with tension, the silence punctuated only by the harsh sounds of their struggle—grunts of exertion, the crack of branches underfoot, and the sickening thud of flesh meeting flesh. Both combatants bore the marks of their clash: gashes that oozed, fur matted with the evidence of their relentless attacks, and gaping bite wounds that spoke of the ferocity with which they sought dominance. Yet, despite the injuries that would have felled lesser creatures, neither Alpha nor Scarback succumbed to the pain. They fought on, their actions guided not by blind animalistic instinct but by a keen acumen.

The macaques' battle was a dance of death and dominance, a brutal ballet that underscored the stakes of their coexistence with humanity. As the minutes stretched on, the outcome of the fight became a tangible thing, hanging in the balance. When the opportunity presented itself, Alpha struck with unerring precision, his teeth sinking into the vulnerable flesh of Scarback's throat—a move that could end the conflict in an instant.

Rather than delivering the killing stroke that millions of years of evolution demanded, Alpha released his grip once submission was clearly established. He maintained a threatening position while allowing his defeated opponent to assume an appropriate subordination posture—a decision that demonstrated a sophisticated understanding beyond simple victory toward a strategic assessment of faction reunification rather than elimination of opposing leadership.

The reaction throughout the surrounding woodland was instantaneous and revealing. Scarback's group dropped their weapons and took up non-threatening stances while Alpha's security contingent stayed alert without exploiting their advantage. The behavioral change mirrored military units acknowledging a transfer of command rather than instinctive animal dominance readjustments—additional proof of something unparalleled in the evolutionary record.

Following Scarback's complete submission, Alpha executed definitive signals that triggered synchronized repositioning of both groups. His protection detail maintained a defensive formation around the negotiation space, while others established a peaceful boundary facing human forces—cohesion restored through combat but directed toward diplomatic continuation, rather than subjugation.

"Stand down to defensive posture only," Harding instructed all security teams, relief and continued vigilance warring in his chest. "Maintain perimeter containment but cease active engagement unless

directly threatened. Medical teams prepare to receive injured if negotiation team requires extraction."

In the clearing, Alpha returned to where Kira waited. Despite blood
matting his fur, he moved with ease and confidence, resuming the
symbolic communication about territorial boundaries—picking up
negotiations as if the factional conflict had never threatened to derail
everything.

"He's reestablishing contact," Elijah reported through the radio.
"He's prioritizing negotiation over treating his injuries—he clearly
values this potential agreement."

For twenty minutes, Kira and Alpha developed their symbolic negotiation, adjusting arrangements to establish basic rules about territories, resources, and interaction protocols. Macaque forces held
security positions without aggression, while human teams maintained
the perimeter without provocation—two species bridging an evolutionary divide.

"They're creating a framework for coexistence," Elijah radioed,
wonder seeping through his scientific tone. "Territorial divisions, observation zones, resource protocols."

The negotiation concluded with Alpha making final adjustments
to the boundaries, clearly separating macaque territory from human
zones. Kira suggested scientific observation posts, which Alpha accepted with specific modifications regarding access—showing his understanding of the delicate balance needed.

With the framework established, Alpha implemented a conclusion protocol—gathering key documentation while leaving reference
markers intact. He signaled his security team, who began a coordinated withdrawal while maintaining defensive positions, moving deeper
into the preserve like soldiers completing a mission.

"Negotiation accomplished," McKenna reported, her voice tinged with relief. "Alpha is withdrawing while preserving the framework. We've achieved preliminary agreement on boundaries and protocols."

As security maintained their watch, broader implications began to emerge. Cypress Grove had become a first contact scenario with non-human intelligence created through human intervention—a precedent with far-reaching implications.

At least two townspeople had been killed by the macaques, and some of that graphic footage had leaked onto social media platforms. Sheriff Harding slumped, massaging his temples as he contemplated the mountain of paperwork, press inquiries, and grieving families awaiting him. The county had never experienced anything remotely like this—how exactly did one classify intelligent primate attacks in official reports?

For now, though, he would savor this shaky, fragile victory, purchased at considerable cost.

Dawn approached with uncertain promise—not peace but a tentative truce between species united by their capacity for strategic thinking and adaptation. The first golden rays stretched across the eastern sky, illuminating a landscape forever changed by the events of the past twenty-four hours.

Whether this understanding would develop into something sustainable or collapse under the threat of fear and misunderstanding remained painfully uncertain, but a path had been established through negotiation rather than mutual destruction.

The sheriff watched Alpha's retreating form with admiration colored with concern—this intelligent being was both a scientific miracle and a dangerous unknown.

# CHAPTER 17

M cKenna Dubrow studied slides under her microscope with practiced focus. A week of relative calm had followed the negotiation, allowing her and Vivian to set up a makeshift lab in her clinic to research the macaques' cognitive enhancement. Though the Cypress Grove Animal Clinic still bore scars from multiple raids, Sheriff Harding's deputies had helped restore essential functions, transforming the damaged exam room into a workable research space.

The fragile truce established through Kira's unprecedented contact had held, though skepticism ran deep throughout the town. Residents stayed vigilant despite the halt in macaque attacks, their collective trauma leaving wounds that would take a very long time to heal.

The rest of Earl Simmons' body hadn't been found yet, but Harold Peterson's funeral had been held three days earlier—a somber reminder of the human cost their community had paid during the confrontation.

"Mom?" Kira's voice came from the clinic doorway, interrupting McKenna's scientific focus. "Elijah just called from the community center. The state officials want everyone there for a meeting in an hour."

McKenna looked up from her microscope, tucking a strand of flax-colored hair behind her ear. She'd seen so many changes in her daughter over the past week. Kira had transformed since becoming the cross-species go-between—her expressions showed new maturity, her attention to detail had sharpened, and most striking, she'd taken a genuine interest in scientific concepts that seemed to have replaced her fashion design obsession.

"Tell him we'll be there," McKenna replied, carefully storing the tissue samples before removing her lab coat.

McKenna packed away her notes, her mind drifting to yesterday's tense call with Martin. Third conversation this week, same pattern—initial concern followed by convenient excuses about why he couldn't leave his research post in Kenya. The macaque crisis had made international news, and Cypress Grove's name was splashed across headlines worldwide. He'd had seen it all, called frantically, then concluded that since the immediate danger had passed, his physical presence wasn't "essential."

Outside the clinic window, she spotted another news van crawling by. They'd become as common as the macaques had once been in town. Three networks had offered exclusive interviews, two magazines wanted photo spreads, and some Hollywood producer had left seven voicemails about rights to their story. McKenna deleted them all.

What Kira needed wasn't cameras and questions but stability. Structure. A mother who wasn't constantly juggling scientific breakthroughs with community trauma. McKenna had started enforcing dinner at six, homework by seven, and limited discussion of macaque matters after eight. Small attempts at normalcy in a situation that was anything but normal.

Kira had spent the week working with Elijah to document and expand the symbolic language they had established with Alpha, creating more sophisticated representational frameworks for potential future negotiations. Her teenage adaptability had indeed proven crucial in understanding the macaques' non-verbal communication methods, while Elijah's scientific rigor provided essential structure, but it couldn't be daily. McKenna was drawing lines.

\* \* \*

The acrid scent of fear-sweat hung in the community center's stale air as McKenna entered. Residents clustered in nervous knots, their eyes darting toward windows that framed empty rooftops—spaces where intelligent, ruthless watchers had once perched. The polished linoleum squeaked under her boots, each step echoing off walls that had never contained a crisis quite like this.

Four strangers commanded the center table, their pressed suits and rigid postures signifying the authority of the federal government.

"Federal wildlife management," Elijah murmured beside her. "Plus military oversight. The APEX files triggered something."

McKenna's jaw clenched. She'd known this moment would come—the bureaucratic machinery grinding toward its inevitable conclusion.

Mayor Holden's voice cut through the murmur, introducing their visitors with the careful diplomacy of someone walking a tightrope. Regional Director Chandler stepped forward, her silver hair catching the harsh fluorescent light. Behind the weathered features lay the cold efficiency of someone who'd spent decades reducing complex situations to simple solutions.

"Standard protocols mandate complete elimination," Chandler announced, her words dropping into the room like stones into still water. "Non-native primates presenting public safety threats require comprehensive removal with specimen preservation for analysis."

The clinical language couldn't mask the brutality underneath. McKenna tasted copper—she'd bitten her tongue.

"These macaques have demonstrated unprecedented cognitive capabilities," she interrupted, scientific credentials lending weight to her words. "They've developed symbolic communication, strategic planning, territorial negotiation. This isn't standard wildlife management—it's first contact."

Colonel Landon studied her with calculating eyes, his military bearing sharp as a straight razor. "Dr. Dubrow, these subjects represent the continuation of research officially terminated decades ago. Security protocols supersede scientific curiosity."

The room closed in around her. They were discussing genocide with the indifferent efficiency of filing paperwork.

"The research potential is extraordinary," Elijah pressed, academic passion overriding caution. "Intelligence developing along non-human pathways—we could be witnessing evolution in real time."

Dr. Thompson from the National Primate Research Center perked up, intrigue flickering beneath her professional mask. "The cognitive enhancement appears epigenetic, accelerated across generations. The study potential under controlled conditions would be invaluable."

Hope sparked in McKenna's chest—a scientist's recognition of unprecedented discovery. "But it's a combination of things... epigenetic, fungal compounds, and scientific tampering. In any case, we've established contact with their leader, Alpha. Territorial boundaries, resource sharing, non-aggression treaties. We could create a protected research preserve, maintain public safety through proper containment."

Chandler's expression remained granite-hard. "These animals have killed. They've systematically attacked infrastructure and injured dozens. Risk assessment doesn't accommodate research fantasies when lives are at stake."

Sheriff Harding's hands cut through the air in frustration. "Your standard protocols failed spectacularly. These aren't ordinary animals—they adapt faster than we can contain them. They must be studied, as Dr. Dubrow and Dr. Jackson say."

The officials exchanged uncomfortable glances. Military precision meeting evolutionary wildcard—and losing.

Kira's voice sliced through the bureaucratic fog with unfiltered clarity. "They don't want war. Alpha made that clear—they just want to exist without being murdered for being different."

Dr. Thompson leaned forward, scientific hunger overriding protocol. "So, it's true? You established actual communication with them?"

Kira nodded.

"Spatial symbols for territory," Elijah explained. "Defensive boundaries, not offensive expansion."

McKenna seized the opening. "Research preserve. Controlled boundaries, monitored development. We study unprecedented cognitive evolution while maintaining public safety."

"I promised them," Kira pleaded.

Elijah nodded, academic enthusiasm crackling. "We've already negotiated preliminary territorial agreements. This could revolutionize our understanding of intelligence emergence."

Chandler's granite expression didn't soften. "They've killed. Injured dozens. Risk assessment doesn't accommodate scientific fantasy."

McKenna's pulse quickened—the moment of truth. "With the help of my colleague, Dr. Vivian Santos," she indicated with a quick

glance at Viv, who was seated nearby, "I've identified the enhancement compound. Fungal-derived neurochemicals that boost cognitive
function. We can kill the mushrooms that are still growing. With
outside help, we can create a counteragent—gradual reduction over
generations, not immediate cognitive collapse."

The room fell silent except for the buzzing lights.

"Controlled regression," Colonel Landon translated, military
mind processing implications. "Slow descent rather than execution."

"Eight to ten generations," McKenna confirmed, her voice steady
despite the ethical vertigo. "Each generation slightly less enhanced
until they return to standard macaque parameters." The moral weight
settled like lead in her stomach. Deliberately reducing intelligence in
another species—but the alternatives were extinction or warfare.

Justin Reeves spoke up, his environmental absolutism tempered
by captivity. "Before they held me, I'd have demanded complete protection. But intelligence without ethical constraint..." He shuddered.
"Dr. Dubrow's approach is the most humane and *sane* option."

Mayor Holden's political instincts kicked in, sensing opportunity
in crisis. "A research preserve brings employment, tourism revenue.
Cypress Grove becomes the center of evolutionary study instead of a
wildlife management disaster."

Director Chandler's voice cut through the tension, loud and clear.
"Contingent upon comprehensive security and regulatory oversight,
we authorize experimental research and your preservation approach."

McKenna's relief tasted tinny, contaminated by the knowledge of
what they'd really agreed to do.

The afternoon dissolved into working groups and implementation
plans, bureaucracy grinding forward with mechanical inevitability.
McKenna found Kira hunched over charts with Elijah, her daughter's
usually soft, rounded teenage features sharp with purpose.

"You okay?"

Kira looked up, something ancient flickering behind adolescent eyes. "The territorial boundaries have to be perfect. One misunderstanding and everything falls apart."

*When did my daughter become this person?* McKenna wondered, parental pride wrestling with the unsettling realization that crisis had carved away childhood, leaving something harder underneath.

By evening, the framework existed—federal resources, security perimeters, monitoring protocols. All very civilized. All very humane. All very much like building a prettier cage.

Dr. Thompson materialized beside her as the meeting dissolved, both women watching sunset paint the reinforced windows crimson. "You realize what we're undertaking," she said, professional directness cutting straight to the moral bone. "Deliberately lobotomizing another species raises some rather uncomfortable questions."

McKenna's laugh emerged bitter and sharp. "As opposed to genocide? Or letting enhanced predators develop without ethical constraints?" She shook her head. "We created this problem. Now we're choosing our preferred method of solving it."

"Science often navigates without moral GPS," Thompson acknowledged. "Especially when we're cleaning up our own accidents."

Sheriff Harding approached, fatigue etched into every line of his sunburned face. "Federal teams establish perimeter tonight. Comprehensive monitoring starts tomorrow."

"Any movement from our enhanced neighbors?"

"Cooper's tracking shows observation posts maintained at agreed boundaries. No territorial violations. Alpha seems to be keeping his word." Harding paused, something troubling flickering across his expression. "For now."

The unspoken truth floated between them like smoke—intelligence without shared evolution created inherent instability. They were all improvising, hoping temporary agreements could bridge the gap between species until the counteragent gradually erased the problem generation by generation.

McKenna pocketed her research notes, the ethical compromise settling into her bones. Tomorrow they'd begin the delicate work of managed extinction—not with bullets or poison, but with chemical whispers that would slowly steal away consciousness across decades.

# CHAPTER 18

McKenna stood motionless before the observation glass, her breath fogging the pristine surface as she watched the sanctuary's newest macaque infants tumble through their morning routines. The scent of disinfectant couldn't quite mask the earthy musk that clung to everything in this place—a reminder that beneath all the gleaming equipment and careful protocols, they were still dealing with wild things trying to remember how to be wild again.

Thirteen months into what the government had christened with the bland bureaucratic title "Cypress Grove Primate Research Preserve," the data was beginning to tell its story in graphs and neural scans that made her hands shake with something between relief and giddiness. The infant brains were developing differently—measurably, quantifiably divergent from their enhanced elders. Their little skulls, soft and malleable as clay, contained ordinary monkey business: territorial squabbles over fruit, grooming rituals older than human civilization, simple territorial displays. Not the disturbing human-adjacent intelligence that had nearly brought Cypress Grove to its knees in those final, blood-soaked days.

"It's working," she whispered to herself, the words tasting like victory seasoned with exhaustion. Her reflection stared back from the glass, hollow-eyed but determined.

The gleaming research facility that surrounded her was a far cry from the blood-spattered wreckage of her clinic after the siege. Amazing what a few million in federal funding could buy when the military suddenly took interest in your work—when your laboratory disasters became matters of national security. The sterile corridors with their state-of-the-art equipment and floor-to-ceiling observation windows felt like atonement wrapped in scientific legitimacy, all chrome surfaces and softly humming machinery. They'd built her a palace to dismantle what humans had created, a monument to the delicate art of undoing enhancement.

Her clinic still stood, and it was back to its former structure and stature. However, Vivian Santos took primary supervision of the day-to-day pet and farm animal care, alongside a recently graduated veterinarian they'd hired.

The fluorescent lighting cast everything in surgical brightness, making the green canopy visible through the windows seem impossibly vivid by contrast—Florida's swampland reclaiming what had always belonged to it.

"Mom." Kira's voice pulled her from the microscope, sharp and businesslike in a way that still caught McKenna off-guard. "Alpha's on the move. Team Two says his group is heading toward the northern boundary. Observation Post Three will have visual in about ten minutes."

McKenna glanced up at her daughter—this phoenix who had emerged from the ashes of the macaque conflict transformed into someone she barely recognized. The girl who once spent hours sketching fashion designs now moved with the precise efficiency of a field researcher, her notebooks filled with meticulous documentation of primate communication patterns instead of evening gown silhouettes. Gone were the New York design school applications, replaced by behavioral charts and interaction matrices. Trauma did that sometimes—rewired neural pathways like some cosmic electrician, created new obsessions from the fragments of shattered dreams.

"Thanks, honey. Let Elijah know, would you? He's been tracking their patrol patterns."

The familiar sound of approaching footsteps on vinyl tile announced his arrival before Kira could move. Elijah Jackson had stayed, of course—career academics didn't walk away from the scientific equivalent of a supernova, and this was exactly that: a once-in-a-lifetime chance to observe intelligence being methodically unraveled. His university had practically shoved him out the door with extended research leave when they realized what they had access to—the world's only population of neurologically enhanced primates gradually being un-enhanced through McKenna's careful, patient treatment.

His perfectly maintained appearance—that immaculate afro despite the humidity that turned everyone else into wilted flowers, those perpetually unwrinkled button-downs that seemed to mock Florida's vengeful climate—had become a reassuring constant in their new reality. Even now, clipboard in hand and pen clicking in that nervous rhythm she'd come to associate with his deeper thoughts, he looked like he'd stepped out of a university catalog rather than a containment facility.

But it was the way he looked at her lately that had changed everything. Not with the clinical interest of a colleague or the careful distance of a fellow survivor, but with something warmer, more exploratory. Something that made her catch her breath when their hands brushed over shared data sheets, something that flickered in the spaces between professional conversations about neuroplasticity and behavioral modification.

They were starting something, she realized—tentatively, carefully, like two people who'd learned that the world could shatter without warning but were brave enough to hope it might also heal. Whatever was growing between them felt fragile as new growth, but it was growing nonetheless, taking root in the fertile ground of shared purpose and mutual understanding. In quiet moments between observations, when Kira was busy with her own research and the sanctuary hummed with the peaceful sounds of recovering minds, McKenna found herself thinking that maybe—just maybe—some enhancements were worth keeping after all.

McKenna gathered her notes and headed toward the northern observation post, passing through the facility's central hub. The place hummed with the quiet industry of scientists who'd found their unicorn. Researchers from primatology, evolutionary biology, neuroscience, linguistics—all circling the macaques with the reverent hunger of pilgrims at a miracle. What had begun in blood and terror had transformed into academic currency of the highest order.

Outside, the unseasonably hot May hit like a wet furnace. The carefully maintained path to Observation Post Three threaded through dense vegetation—civilization's tentative thread through wilderness. They'd designed it to be just visible enough for humans while minimally troubling to the macaques. There was an underground electric fence that kept the monkeys contained. A compromise, like everything about the sanctuary.

Sheriff Harding—no, *Security Director* Harding now—stood at the observation post, khaki-clad and vigilant. The siege had changed him too, pulled him from small-town law enforcement into something more complex. He'd found purpose in this new border between species, his considerable experience finally serving something more significant than drunk drivers and domestic disputes.

"Morning, McKenna," he nodded, a tight smile crossing his features. "Alpha's group spotted about fifteen minutes ago—standard formation, moving along the northern border. They're carrying botanical samples. More of those fungi they've been harvesting."

McKenna nodded, her stomach tightening involuntarily at the mention of the fungi. The chemical precursors to Compound P-17—the substance that had accelerated their cognitive development. "They're still collecting them. Whether for consumption or study, I can't say."

The observation post provided a commanding view of the northern sanctuary, with high-powered optics bringing distant movements into sharp clarity. Through the scope, McKenna could see Alpha's group moving with their signature efficiency—the purposeful progress of beings with agenda and method.

Elijah joined them moments later, tablet ready to document. "Alpha's been changing their patrol patterns," he noted, scrolling through previous observations. "Same territory coverage, but different timing, different group compositions. Adapting to our observation routines, perhaps. Or responding to resource distribution changes."

Through the scope, Alpha himself came into view, his scarred face and filmy eye instantly recognizable. Several months of relative peace hadn't dulled the primitive jolt of fear that shot through McKenna's chest at the sight of him. Some nightmares don't fade with daylight. The intelligence behind that damaged eye had orchestrated killing, calculated strategy, and manipulated humans like game pieces. That he now operated within negotiated boundaries didn't erase what they'd seen him do.

"His communication complexity hasn't diminished despite the treatment implementation," Elijah observed, noting the macaque's gestures through the scope. "The effects seem concentrated in newborns and juveniles, not adults with established neural pathways."

Just as they'd designed it. Their treatment didn't lobotomize the enhanced adults—ethically indefensible and practically suicidal—but prevented the neurochemical processes that supported enhanced development in new births. Kinder to prevent intelligence than to take it away, they'd told themselves. Easier to justify, at least.

As they watched, Alpha's group unexpectedly altered course, moving toward the sanctuary border near their observation post. McKenna felt her heart rate kick up a notch, the body remembering siege days before the mind could reassure it. Then she saw what Alpha carried—a small form clutched against his chest, a baby macaque held with protective care.

"They're approaching the interaction zone," Harding said, vigilance clicking into place.

The interaction zone—their diplomatic border crossing, established after months of tentative experiments. As Alpha reached the boundary, his intent became clear. The juvenile he carried had suffered a compound fracture to its right leg, the bone visibly misaligned under the skin.

"He's coming for medical assistance," McKenna noted. Throughout the sanctuary's establishment, they'd maintained strict non-intervention regarding internal colony events. Alpha's decision to bring an injured child to them represented trust, perhaps. Or calculation. With Alpha, the line between the two remained blurry.

"I need to respond," she said, reaching for the emergency medical kit. The scientist in her saw valuable data; the doctor saw a patient; the survivor saw Alpha's watching eye, evaluating her response.

McKenna approached the boundary with the careful movements she'd use with any wild animal, though this, of course, was no ordinary wild animal. Alpha watched her approach, his good eye tracking her movements with an assessment that transcended instinct.

At the boundary line, Alpha placed the injured juvenile on a flat rock, then stepped back precisely two meters—close enough to protect, far enough to allow work. The gesture conveyed more meaning than any spoken language could have: *Help this one. I will wait. I am watching.*

McKenna's veterinary training took over as she examined the juvenile. Clean fracture of tibia and fibula, likely from a fall. She spoke as she worked, explaining her actions with words Alpha couldn't understand and gestures he somehow did.

"I need to set the bone and immobilize it. This will hurt, but it's necessary for proper healing."

Alpha's response chilled her. He made specific gestures to his security macaques, establishing a perimeter, then reached out to hold the juvenile's upper body in a perfect restraint position—exactly as a human nurse might stabilize a human child during a procedure.

Working with steady hands that betrayed none of her inner turmoil, McKenna set the fractured bones and applied a lightweight composite cast. Throughout the procedure, Alpha maintained his hold, adjusting the pressure in response to her nonverbal cues, much like a seasoned medical assistant.

After completing the treatment, McKenna stepped back across the boundary line, distance as ritual and reassurance. Alpha gathered the patient, examining the cast with evident comprehension before making a precise gesture they'd documented as acknowledgment. His group withdrew in formation, the entire encounter lasting just twenty-two minutes but shattering months of scientific assumptions.

"That was extraordinary," Elijah breathed as they returned to the observation post. "Deliberate medical assistance-seeking. Cross-species trust development. Risk-benefit assessment."

"More than that," McKenna said, the implications spreading like ripples in her mind. "He specifically sought *me*—not any human, but the one with medical knowledge. He didn't just know they needed help; he knew exactly what kind of help and who could provide it."

Back at the research facility, the incident detonated like a philosophical bomb among the scientific teams. Dr. Thompson from the National Primate Research Center practically vibrated with excitement, ice melting in her soda as she gestured wildly during the afternoon briefing.

"This demonstrates sophisticated theory of mind," she insisted, the fluorescent lights catching the gleam in her eyes. "Not just recognizing that others have knowledge, but categorizing specialized knowledge and seeking its specific application. We're witnessing cognitive architecture that exceeds our documented parameters—for enhanced primates *and* natural ones."

The sterile conference room suddenly felt smaller, charged with the electricity of implications.

Dr. Rivera, the federal oversight representative whose job description read like a diplomatic minefield, cut to the ethical heart with surgical precision. "Does this interaction require us to reconsider our transition approach? If they're demonstrating cooperative strategies rather than purely competitive ones, is cognitive reduction still ethically justified?"

The question hung in the recycled air like a live grenade with the pin already pulled. Their entire approach—months of careful planning, millions in federal funding, McKenna's reputation—rested on the premise that enhanced macaque intelligence without human ethical frameworks created dangerous incompatibility. But cooperation? Cooperation challenged that premise at its very foundation, like finding cracks in the laws of physics.

"One cooperative interaction doesn't erase what happened during the siege," Harding countered, his background overriding philosophical niceties. "Alpha implemented sophisticated tactical operations that killed people. Those capabilities remain intact despite peaceful interactions now."

McKenna felt the familiar weight of ethical quicksand pulling her under. The macaques hadn't asked for enhancement; military researchers had gifted them capabilities without bothering to consider the consequences. Yet, uncontrolled development of predator intelligence without ethical constraints? That created risks no one was prepared to manage.

The perfect lose-lose scenario, wrapped in government funding and academic legitimacy.

"We continue as established," she decided after watching her colleagues chase their tails through circular arguments.

\* \* \*

Evening found her in the observation room with Kira, watching footage of the interaction while shadows crept across the facility like dark thoughts made manifest. Her daughter studied the video with the intensity of someone trying to decode the universe's cruelest joke, cataloging Alpha's gestures with the precision of a linguist working with humanity's last undiscovered language.

"Do you think they understand what we're doing to them?" Kira asked suddenly, her question slicing through scientific distance to expose the moral nerve underneath. "That we're gradually making them... less than what they are now?"

McKenna's parental autopilot kicked in—*lie to protect her*—before her scientist's integrity overrode the impulse. Kira had earned the right to navigate this ethical minefield as an adult.

"I believe Alpha understands more than we might expect," she admitted, tasting the bitter complexity of truth. "Whether he comprehends the specific neurological mechanisms or just perceives general population changes over time... we'll see."

Kira went home, and McKenna completed her documentation while watching security teams conduct evening patrols along the boundary—armed guards protecting both sides from each other. What had begun in blood and fear had evolved into something resembling stability. Not peace exactly, but the absence of open warfare.

Movement at the preserve boundary caught her attention through the reinforced glass. A distinctive silhouette briefly visible in security lighting before deliberately melting into vegetation with predatory grace. Alpha, watching beyond his standard patrol routes, intelligence operating through evolutionary pathways humans might never fully comprehend, despite their extensive efforts.

McKenna watched Alpha's dark form disappear into the darkness. The fragile equilibrium they'd established felt suddenly precarious, balanced on the edge of understanding that might be withdrawn at any moment. The preserve's careful geographic division had been their saving grace these past months—Alpha's colony claiming the northern territories while Scarback's group maintained dominance in the southern reaches. A cold war of sorts, neither leader encroaching on the other's domain. Their mutual hatred remained palpable even across kilometers of separation, yet both had apparently calculated that open conflict served neither colony's interests.

An uneasy truce, maintained through distance rather than reconciliation. McKenna had documented their border behaviors obsessively—the territorial displays at boundary zones, the elaborate warning systems both colonies had established. Sometimes she wondered if their shared experience of human manipulation had created this temporary alliance of convenience.

She turned from the window, rubbing her temples. How long before the compound's effects altered this delicate balance? Would diminished intelligence in the younger generation eventually erode the strategic thinking that currently prevented all-out war? And if it did, would that make them safer, or simply more unpredictable?

McKenna closed her journal with that understanding crystallizing into something that felt less like acceptance and more like surrender to forces beyond her comprehension. The line between human intelligence and animal instinct hadn't just blurred through military meddling—it had been obliterated, creating an evolutionary branch that perhaps was *always* meant to exist, just waiting for the right catalyst to emerge from humanity's darker impulses.

# Epilogue

The setting sun bled through the leaves, painting everything in amber and gold. Alpha sat motionless in the cypress tree, his muscles relaxed but ready. The rough bark pressed against his calloused hands and feet, familiar and grounding. From here, he could see the human place—the research building with its strange, clear walls that let him look inside but kept him outside.

He tracked the humans moving in their light-box. The female—McKenna—bent over her seeing-machine. The male—Elijah—brought her water. Alpha's damaged eye saw only shapes and shadows through a fuzzy haze, but his good eye missed nothing. His nostrils flared, catching the evening scents—decaying leaves, stagnant puddles, the musky odor of his own kind in the distance, and the faint chemical smell that always surrounded the human place.

Two years since the fighting stopped. Two years of watching, planning, waiting. The invisible line they'd drawn between his territory and theirs had held. What they called "protocols" worked well enough. Their "Cypress Grove Primate Research Preserve" gave his colony space to live without human hunters pointing their bang-sticks.

Alpha's mind worked differently now than before the changes started. The special plants that had woken his thoughts still grew in secret places throughout his territory. He still ate them, still felt their power spreading through his blood and lighting up dark corners of his mind. But something was happening to the young ones born after the humans started putting the tasteless thing in the water.

The babies grew wrong. Their eyes lacked the spark. They learned slower, forgot faster, followed instinct more than thought. Alpha knew this without understanding exactly how the humans did it. He saw the effect without knowing its cause. The female had done something to make his kind less like her kind over time. Not taking away what he had, but making sure the new ones never got it.

He'd allowed this because fighting would have meant death. The humans had their bang-sticks and their burning-things and their endless numbers. His colony had speed and strength and cleverness, but not enough. The territory they'd claimed let his colony live and grow, even if the youngest ones would never know the full light of thought that he enjoyed.

Below, the transparent walls showed him the two-legs, McKenna and Elijah, moving together in ways that had changed over the seasons. They still came to the edge of the green, sometimes. Alpha observed them from the high branches, noting the subtle shifts in their scent, the way their furless hands brushed, the soft sounds they made to each other. He recognized the bonding rituals, the intricate dance of connection that mirrored his own troop's complex social web. They were not threats, not now. They were simply... paired. He understood the need for connection, for shared purpose.

His friend, Kira, visited less often. Her scent still carried the familiar sweetness of ripe berries and sunshine, but now it was overlaid with other, fainter traces—the metallic tang of the two-leg city to the south, the crisp scent of manufactured cloth, the subtle musk of other, younger two-legs. Her responsibilities had shifted, her attention drawn elsewhere. Alpha accepted this. Change was the current that shaped the green, and even the two-legs were not immune.

The noisy, banner-waving two-legs were gone. Their scents had faded from the wind, their insistent calls silenced. They had served their purpose, a brief distraction in the larger game. Alpha did not mourn their absence. They had been... inefficient. Sentimentality was a weakness, a vulnerability that could be exploited. Survival demanded pragmatism, a clear-eyed assessment of threats and opportunities.

Alpha's fingers tightened on the branch, remembering the weight of weapons they'd once held during the war. Tools that he'd taught others to use. The young ones born before the humans' water-change still learned quickly, still held the spark in their eyes. He'd made sure these special ones learned everything he knew—how to make and use tools, how to read the markings humans made, how to plan and remember and think beyond hunger and fear.

Alpha slid down the tree trunk, the rough bark scraping pleasantly against his calloused palms. The night sounds rose around him—frogs singing their mating calls, insects buzzing, night birds beginning their hunts. His ears caught them all, building a sound-map of the world that was as clear as what his eyes showed him.

He moved through the darkening forest with sure, silent steps. His feet knew every root and hole without looking. His time in this new territory had been enough to learn it completely. His colony no longer ran in fear or fought for survival. They built sleeping places. They stored food. They planned for seasons not yet come. They lived as neither fully macaque nor human, but something in between.

Near the edge of the invisible line, Alpha stopped and dug behind a thorny bush, ignoring the scratches on his arms. His fingers found the smooth artificial vine he'd taken from the human place during the fighting times. He'd kept it hidden, waiting for the right time to use it.

The feel of it brought memories flooding back—the taste of fear in his mouth as his colony fought the humans, the burning in his lungs as he ran through smoke and noise, the warm stickiness of blood on his hands. The vine felt cool and wrong against his skin, not like the natural things of his world.

With practiced movements, his fingers twisted and looped the vine into a complex shape that he'd seen in one of the humans' picture-carriers. But he added his own patterns, his own meaning. When finished, the knot resembled nothing in nature—too ordered, too intentional—a thing made by a mind that shouldn't exist in his kind.

Alpha breathed in deeply, tasting the night air. The scent of the human place carried to him on the breeze—sharp cleaning-smells, machine-oil, and the particular perfume-smell of McKenna that he'd come to recognize over months of watching. He placed the knot exactly where the morning humans would find it when they walked their same path as they did when the sun was new.

The knot could mean many things. A warning. A greeting. A reminder. The humans would argue about its meaning, never agreeing, never understanding fully. But they would know it came from him, and they would know he was still watching. Still thinking. Still planning.

As darkness wrapped around the forest, Alpha moved silently toward where a special young one waited by the hidden entrance to the underground place. This young one—born to Scarback's mate but now loyal to Alpha since the fight that settled who would lead—had shown the quick-learning that marked those born before the water-change.

The young one had dug a perfect hiding place beneath tangled roots, following Alpha's teaching exactly. Inside this earth-pocket, they now placed the treasures Alpha had gathered over months—sharp metal things taken from human places, picture-carriers with markings showing the territory, stones arranged in patterns that told stories without sounds. Knowledge that would sleep in the ground until needed.

Similar hiding places lay scattered throughout Alpha's territory, each holding pieces of what his kind had learned. Things that wouldn't be forgotten even when the new ones born without the spark became more numerous. Seeds of knowledge planted in the earth, waiting.

Alpha watched from the shadows as the young one finished covering the hiding place with leaves and twigs, making it invisible to careless eyes. The smell of fresh earth and crushed plants filled his nostrils. The young one's movements showed understanding beyond instinct—careful, precise, thoughtful. This one would teach others when Alpha was gone.

When darkness fully claimed the forest, Alpha returned to the colony's sleeping place. From his high resting spot, he could just make out the distant lights of the human town beyond their territory. The humans there went about their small lives, never knowing how close they'd come to something they couldn't understand. Never knowing that Alpha had considered options that would have left their town empty and silent.

The humans believed they'd solved their problem. Their tests showed the young ones growing more normal, more predictable, less dangerous with each new birth. McKenna's water-change was working, slowly making his kind into what humans thought they should be—simple animals without the burden and danger of real thought.

But the humans didn't understand what Alpha had hidden throughout the territory. They didn't know about the secret gardens where the special plants still grew, tended carefully by those he'd taught. They hadn't found the hiding places with tools and knowledge waiting for the right time. They couldn't see that Alpha wasn't just accepting their arrangement—he was adapting to it, planning beyond it.

As sleep approached, Alpha's mind filled with images and plans. The peace between his kind and the humans worked for now. It gave both sides what they needed most—safety, territory, time. The humans got to study and control. His colony got to live and prepare.

But Alpha had seen inside the human buildings. He'd watched their moving-picture-boxes. He'd learned from the markings in their knowledge-holders. He knew about the bigger world beyond this small territory, about the endless human places spreading across the earth. He understood that humans forgot quickly, that what happened here would fade from their minds as seasons passed.

The knot he'd left would remind them—for now. It would tell them he was still thinking, still watching, still planning beyond what they could see. It was a joke, a tease.

As consciousness faded into sleep, Alpha's mind held one last thought—a simple truth the humans never fully grasped. The water-change might work on the new ones, but those already changed would live many seasons more. They would preserve what they knew. They would wait. And one day, when the humans had forgotten to be afraid, when their vigilance had faded like morning mist...

Alpha's good eye closed while his damaged one remained partly open, giving him the appearance of watching even in slumber. Outside, the night creatures fell suddenly silent as something moved through the darkness. Inside the colony's sleeping place, soft clicks and hoots passed between sentries—not random animal sounds but a language no human had fully decoded.

Peace existed because Alpha allowed it to exist.

For now.

# AFTERWORD

There are several more *Nature's Nightmares* books in the works, so if you'd like to be kept in the loop, please visit StaciLayneWilson.com

Special thanks to Linda Rose and Janice Andrews. Plus a shout-out to the best veterinarian ever, Dr. Sean McCluskey of Island Pet Hospital in Las Vegas, Nevada!

If you liked this book, please kindly rate and review... indie authors depend on word of mouth (or word of fingertips, as the case may be). Thank you!

**Staci Layne Wilson** enjoys writing about herself in the third person, and playing with her pet dumbo rats. She is an L.A. native who enjoys traffic, wildfires, and earthquakes—but since her move to Las Vegas, she's learned to love 110-degree summers, drive-thru wedding chapels, and casinos that still reek of the Rat Pack's cigars. She has been a professional writer since the age of twelve, when she was hired as a columnist for a national magazine. When she's not writing books, she's making movies (*Cabaret of the Dead, The Ventures: Stars on Guitars, The Second Age of Aquarius*, and *Dark House of the Mannequins*).